Match Wits with The Hardy Boys®!

Collect the Original
Hardy Boys Mystery Stories®
by Franklin W. Dixon

Celebrate 60 Years with the World's Greatest Super Sleuths!

THE JUNGLE PYRAMID

GOLD bullion—a million dollars worth—has been stolen from the Wakefield Mint under strange circumstances. Mr. Hardy is asked to investigate but before long his life is threatened, and he asks Frank and Joe to help him.

The boys fly to Zurich, Switzerland, hoping to get information at the Swiss Gold Syndicate and to find the man who has stolen a valuable ancient gold figurine from a New York museum. Their search on both counts seems futile. They return to the United States, where they uncover new clues that take them to Mexico and a breathtaking adventure at an archaeological dig in the Yucatán jungle.

But the Hardys' travels lead to nothing but new doubts and nagging suspicions. And now their lives are in danger. Their adversaries are cunning, elusive, and determined to eliminate Mr. Hardy, and the boys too!

Events culminate in a surprising revelation when their enemies are finally outsmarted by the Hardys.

"Help—me!" Joe yelled.

The Hardy Boys Mystery Stories®

THE
JUNGLE
PYRAMID

BY

FRANKLIN W. DIXON

GROSSET & DUNLAP
Publishers • New York
A member of The Putnam & Grosset Group

PRINTED ON RECYCLED PAPER

CONTENTS

THE
JUNGLE
PYRAMID

CHAPTER I

Gold Heist

FRANK Hardy turned the controls of a stereo set. "I'll see if I can find some country music, Joe," he said to his brother. "Waiting for Dad to phone about a new mystery gives me the jitters."

"Same here," said Joe. "I wonder why he didn't tell us anything about the case he's on."

"It must be top secret."

The Hardy boys were sons of Fenton Hardy, a private detective who worked out of Bayport since retiring from the New York Police Department. Dark-haired Frank was eighteen. Joe was blond and a year younger. Their father had taught them most of what he knew about crime detection, and they sometimes helped him with his investigations but often took cases of their own.

A Kentucky hoedown came over the stereo, and a nasal voice sang the "Blue Grass Blues."

Joe was lying on the floor, his hands cupped

behind his head. "It's just as well that Mother and Aunt Gertrude are out shopping." He chuckled. "This isn't their beat."

The country-western rhythm rose to a crescendo, then died away. Suddenly footsteps pounded on the front porch of the Hardy home. The door burst open and a plump, freckle-faced youth rushed into the room, clutching a rolled-up paper in one hand. He was Chet Morton, the Hardys' best friend.

"I got it!" he cried. "I got it!"

"Got what, Chet?" Joe demanded.

"My correspondence-course diploma!"

Joe turned off the stereo. "A real one? Well, congratulations."

"What's this diploma for?" Frank asked.

"Collecting more bottle tops than anyone else?" Joe needled their visitor, who always became involved with one hobby after another.

Chet looked pained. "That's kid stuff. I thought you guys were detectives."

"Give us a clue," Joe suggested.

Chet did not reply. Instead he unrolled the paper and held it up for them to see. The words STATE CORRESPONDENCE SCHOOL were blazoned across the top. The diploma certified that Chester Morton was considered adept in gold artifacts, and it was signed by the president of the school.

Chet grinned. "Adept means I'm pretty good with the gold. Go ahead. Ask me questions. Want to know about Aztec masks or—"

The phone shrilled before he could finish his sentence. Frank seized the instrument and canted it away from his ear so the other two could hear. Fenton Hardy was calling.

"Frank, Joe," he said hurriedly, "are you both there?"

"Yes, Dad," Frank answered. "Where are you?"

"I'm in Wakefield. That's a hundred miles from Bayport on the way to New York City. A consignment of gold has been stolen from the mint here. The case is too big for one detective, and I need your help. Come to the Archway Motel. Tell Mother and Aunt Gertrude where you'll be, but don't say there's any danger involved. Make it fast! Ah-ah-aaa—"

Mr. Hardy groaned and ended his sentence in a gasp. Then the boys heard a scuffling noise.

"Dad!" Frank shouted. "Dad, what's going on?"

Something hit the floor with a heavy thump, and there was a dragging sound. A door slammed in the background. Then silence. The three boys stared at one another in dismay.

"What—?" Chet began.

"Sh—sh!" Frank said and motioned to the phone.

Footsteps could be heard approaching. Someone breathing heavily picked up the receiver.

"Hello!" Frank said. "Hello?"

The phone clicked, and the line went dead.

"That wasn't Dad who hung up!" Frank exclaimed. "Something's wrong!"

"That's for sure," Joe said grimly.

"Try the motel desk," Chet suggested.

Frank dialed the Archway Motel and asked for Fenton Hardy's room. A moment later the clerk reported that there was no answer. Frank asked to speak to the manager. He introduced himself, then explained to the man that he had heard strange noises coming from his father's room.

"It sounded as if he were being attacked," Frank concluded.

"Attacked!" the manager exploded. "I'll check immediately and will call you back."

Frank hung up. "What do you make of it?" he asked his brother.

"Somebody must have sneaked up on Dad while he was talking on the phone," Joe said. "Someone he hadn't counted on."

"Probably more than one person," Chet added. "He could have taken care of himself otherwise."

"Not if he were hit by surprise," Joe argued.

The phone shrilled again. Frank picked it up.

"Mr. Hardy's room is empty," the motel manager said. "I've also had him paged, but he doesn't answer."

"Anything wrong in the room?" Frank asked.

"No—except that the bedspread was half pulled off and some clothes were lying on the floor. When I see your father, I'll tell him you called. I'll also notify the police just in case your suspicions are correct." The manager hung up, and so did Frank.

"Dad must have been dragged from the room," the young detective theorized. "That could account for the bedspread. We'd better do something fast!"

"We'll have to go to Wakefield right away!" Joe said.

"How about my going along?" Chet put in. "I know all about gold. Maybe I can identify the loot." Then he added, "As long as it's not too dangerous to handle."

The Hardys were used to Chet's shying away from danger, but they knew they could rely on him when the sleuthing became rough. He had been helpful in many of their investigations.

"Okay, Chet," Joe said. "Call home and we'll be off."

"Leave your jalopy in our garage," Frank suggested. "Better get some clean clothes out of it."

Chet and the Hardys always carried extra clothes in their cars in case of an emergency.

Frank quickly scribbled a note telling his mother and Aunt Gertrude that they were on the way to Wakefield to join Mr. Hardy. He added that there was nothing to worry about. "Not much!" he thought to himself. "Just whether Dad's dead or alive!"

Joe backed the car out of the garage and soon the three boys were rolling down Main Street. Joe fretted at the wheel because traffic was heavy, but finally they got out of the city. He stepped on the gas and they roared toward Wakefield.

Mile after mile zipped away beneath their wheels. They passed farmhouses and pastures. At one spot chickens, out of their coops, fled squawking as the car rocketed by them.

Chet remarked, "If you should run over any of our feathered friends, stop so I can pick some up. Chicken soup is a great dish. I haven't had anything since breakfast but a couple of hamburgers and a bottle of soda."

Food always interested Chet, even in the middle of an investigation. The Hardys usually laughed at his remarks, but this time they said nothing.

"Okay," Chet said, "I get the message. I was just testing. Trying to cheer you up."

"I could use some cheering," Frank admitted. "Do you think Dad's been kidnapped, Joe?"

"I'm afraid so," his brother replied glumly. "Probably by the crooks who were responsible for the gold heist."

"Don't jump to conclusions," Chet advised. "Anyway, your father has always managed to get out of tight spots because he's the smartest detective we know. Right?"

"Right," said Frank and Joe in unison.

"Let's talk about something else," Chet said.

"Like what?" Joe inquired.

"Like gold!" Chet answered. "Do you know the melting point of gold?"

Joe grinned. "Over a thousand degrees centigrade."

Chet looked crestfallen. "Oh, so you know that. Well, what can you dissolve gold with?"

"A mixture of hydrochloric and nitric acid."

"You Hardys know everything," Chet complained.

Frank decided to soothe their friend's feelings. "Not as much as you do, Chet. It's just that we ran some lab tests on gold for one of our clients."

The Hardys had a criminology laboratory over their garage, where they did scientific analyses for their clients. They matched fingerprints under the microscope and carried out chemical tests of poisons, explosives, and other materials from the scene of a crime.

While the boys were talking, they approached a hill with a stone wall on the right. Joe drove up as fast as he could within the speed limit. Suddenly a large station wagon hurtled over the crest of the hill. The driver, a burly man, was hunched over the wheel. He was on the wrong side of the road and raced directly at their car!

"Watch it, Joe!" Frank shouted.

Because of the wall, Joe could not move any farther to the right. With split-second timing, he swerved to the left. The station wagon swept past on the right. The Hardys' car skidded out of control for a moment, but Joe pulled it back into the correct lane and went on.

"Lucky you kept your cool," Frank complimented his brother. "There wasn't enough room for a dime between that station wagon and us."

"You can say that again," Chet remarked. "That knucklehead shouldn't be allowed to drive a kiddie car."

The three settled back for the rest of their trip to Wakefield, and Chet continued his lecture on gold. He described how prehistoric people used the yellow metal for jewelry, such as rings and bracelets, and later for money. He added that currently most of the gold was obtained from the deep mines in South Africa.

"The Russians," Chet revealed, "mine gold in Siberia and sell it on the international market. Headquarters for the gold exchange is Zurich, Switzerland."

"Perhaps the stolen Wakefield gold came originally from Siberia," Joe reasoned. "But who knows whether or not we'll ever see it."

"Talking about gold," Chet informed them, "there's an exhibition at the Early Art Museum in New York. Old Scythian artifacts. I hear it's fabulous."

"Sounds interesting," Joe said. "Maybe we can go there after we find Dad."

He turned left to get off the highway at the Wakefield exit, and ten minutes later drew into the Archway Motel parking lot. The boys went inside, where a teen-age youth stood at the registration desk.

"Any message from Fenton Hardy?" Joe asked him.

"Watch it, Joe!" Frank shouted.

"No. But I have one for Frank and Joe Hardy. Is that you?"

"Yes," Frank replied.

"Somebody called," the clerk stated. "Didn't give his name. Just said for Frank and Joe Hardy to come to the Stacy Hotel."

"How do we get there?" Frank asked.

"Go left to the end of the road, make a right, then another right at the second traffic light. It's a flea-bitten rattrap in a rough neighborhood. Watch your step."

"Will do," Frank said. "And thanks for the tip."

The drive to the Stacy took the boys into an area of run-down houses and dismal streets. Local toughs sauntered by, glowering at them.

"I hope we don't run into street gangs," Chet remarked. "A guy could be mugged in this end of town without half trying."

Joe parked in front of the Stacy. The boys climbed out and stood on the sidewalk, gazing up at the grimy exterior of the hotel. A bewhiskered tramp strolled up the street toward them. He was dressed in old clothes, battered shoes, and a slouch hat. They stepped aside to let him pass.

Abreast of them, the tramp suddenly turned and deliberately bumped into Joe. "Follow me," he snarled, "if you know what's good for you!"

CHAPTER II

The Subterranean Vault

REACTING instinctively, Frank and Joe grabbed the tramp's arms to keep him from pulling a knife or a gun. Chet waved a fist under the man's nose.

"Fellows, hold it!" said a familiar voice. "I'll go quietly."

The tramp was Fenton Hardy! As the boys showed their surprise, he whispered, "Don't give me away. Play my game."

"Okay," Frank replied. "But we're glad to see you." Aloud he said, "All right, Harry, we'll buy your dinner."

He led the way into the hotel, where they sat down at a table in a secluded corner of the dining room. The other customers looked seedy, and the waitress chewed gum loudly as she took their order. When the food arrived, Chet seized his knife and fork and began to eat with gusto.

"I was in my room," Mr. Hardy said in a low tone, "when a couple of men came in—"

He broke off as he noticed that the waitress was still standing near their table, flipping through her order pad. Then he said loudly, "A couple of men came in and asked me if I wanted to buy an encyclopedia."

The waitress went to another table to present the check. Mr. Hardy resumed his story. "They jumped me while I was talking to you on the phone, and slipped a cloth saturated with chloroform over my face."

Frank nodded. "We heard a thud and figured somebody was dragging you out of the room."

"Right. When I came to, I was in an old abandoned garage. I—" Mr. Hardy suddenly changed the subject and talked about finding a job at the Wakefield lumber company, since the waitress again stood within earshot. After she had left, he continued, "That girl seems rather nosey. Well, anyway, I picked the lock, got out, went to my car, and put on this disguise. Then I called the Archway Motel from a pay phone and left the message about meeting me at the Stacy."

"What's it all about?" Frank asked.

"The Wakefield Mint has been robbed of a big consignment of gold bars. The haul is worth over a million dollars!"

Joe whistled. "That's a big deal!"

Mr. Hardy agreed. "I've been hired by John Armstrong, the administrative assistant to the director of the mint. He asked me to keep this secret. That's why I couldn't tell you what the investigation was about. Then I received a threatening phone call warning me to get off the case. At that point, I decided I'd better send you an SOS."

"Good thing you did," Frank said.

Mr. Hardy went on, "Incidentally, Chet, I'm glad you came along. That fist you waved under my nose seems like a mighty lethal weapon."

Chet tried to grin, but was not very successful since his mouth was full of baked potato.

"Got any leads, Dad?" Joe asked.

Fenton Hardy shook his head. "Not really. I assume the pair who chloroformed me belong to the gang that stole the gold. Beyond that, nothing."

Frank and Joe ruminated over their father's experience as they finished the meal. Chet downed his last mouthful of apple pie. As the waitress was adding up the tab, Frank handed his father a ten dollar bill.

"There, Harry, that should help you out for a while," he said.

"Thanks, my boy," Mr. Hardy replied, speaking in the whine of a tramp down on his luck.

Leaving the hotel, he whispered to Frank, "Stay at the Shadyside Motel down the street tonight. Meet me at my car at nine in the morning. It's parked in a private garage at ten Pine Street. The people who own it are away, so I'm using it as my dressing room. I can change my disguises there without being seen."

The elder Hardy slouched away into the darkness, and the boys drove to the Shadyside Motel, where they spent the night. In the morning they met Mr. Hardy as arranged. The detective no longer looked like a tramp. He had stashed the old clothes and the fake whiskers in the trunk of his car and resumed his usual appearance.

"Mr. Hardy, you sure fooled me last night," Chet said.

"That was the idea," the sleuth told him. "If my disguises didn't fool everybody, I'd be in big trouble. Boys, suppose we take your car."

Frank got behind the wheel. "Where to?"

"The Wakefield Mint."

The mint was a square three-story building. Faced with white stone, it had rows of narrow windows along the second story. The ground floor was sheathed in stone and steel.

The foyer inside contained a collection of coins and medals produced by the mint. A crowd milled around the main exhibit, a medal representing John Smith at Jamestown.

Fenton Hardy showed his pass to a guard, who escorted him and the boys down a corridor, through a door lined with steel bars, to the office of the administrative assistant.

John Armstrong was a friendly looking man who wore horn-rimmed glasses. He got up from the swivel chair behind his big desk and shook hands with Mr. Hardy, then with each boy, as he was introduced.

"They've helped me on previous cases," the investigator explained, "and I'll need them to assist me on this one." He described the kidnap attempt.

Armstrong expressed concern, then said he had no objections to the boys' participating. "Perhaps, then, you can solve our problem quicker," he remarked. "I want this case cracked before Director Wadsworth gets back from his vacation. I'm responsible for the mint while he's away, you know."

"Mr. Armstrong, suppose you clue us in," Frank suggested.

Armstrong looked grave. "First, let me remind you that there must be no leaks about the theft. We don't want any publicity in the news media."

"Mum's the word," Chet vowed.

Joe inquired about security precautions.

"The best," Armstrong stated. "See this panel on my desk? It monitors the entire mint. We have hidden television cameras watching every square inch of the building. Our security equipment includes trip wires, photoelectric plates, and laser beams. If anybody gets in their way, sirens go off and warning lights flash on the panel."

"It sounds as if you're better protected than Fort Knox," Joe said. "How come the gold was stolen anyway?"

"That's just it," Armstrong said, looking bewildered. "The equipment must have been turned off. It was back on the next morning, however."

"What about the guards?" Frank asked.

"That's stranger yet," Armstrong went on. "One was posted at the outer door, one at the inner steel door, and one here in my office, monitoring the mint through the TV cameras. They were supposed to alert the rest of the night shift if anything happened, but they didn't."

"In other words, they went off with the thieves," Chet said.

"No. They're here!"

"You mean they helped the thieves get in, then let them escape with the loot, and stayed behind?" Joe was incredulous.

"Yes. That's what's so strange," Armstrong replied. "They claim nothing unusual happened at any time that night. The police questioned them after they were arrested but they're sticking to their story."

Frank shook his head. "It doesn't make sense. Where was the gold taken from?"

"The subterranean vault," Armstrong said. "Come on. I'll take you down there."

He ushered the group to his private elevator and pushed the button. The elevator descended three floors. The doors opened and Armstrong led the way to a steel door, where a guard was on duty. He spun the dial until the combination clicked and pushed the door inward.

The boys gaped. Gold bars about a foot long were stacked in rows on racks that stretched across most of the room. A yellow gleam shimmered under fluorescent lighting. A couple of men in shirtsleeves were counting the bars and entering figures in a ledger.

Chet's eyes bulged. "There's got to be a million dollars in here," he practically shouted.

"More than that, young man," Armstrong said. "We're missing twenty-five bars. Each weighs over twenty-seven pounds, and with gold selling on the international market at a very high rate presently, that consignment comes to more than a million."

He gestured toward an empty rack near the door. "That's where the stolen bars were when we closed the vault for the night. The thieves must have carted the gold out of here and around to the outer door at the rear of the building. That's where they made their getaway."

Frank was peering at the nearest row of gold bars. "Why, they're stamped with the hammer and sickle," he noted.

"Same as the missing gold," Armstrong replied. "The Russians traded it through middlemen in Zurich, who sold it to us."

He conducted them out of the gold room and through the subterranean vault to a freight elevator. They emerged at the rear door of the mint. A guard let them through into a receiving area, where some armored cars were parked.

"I'm late for a meeting," Armstrong said and excused himself. "Please look around all you want and we'll talk later." He went back to his office.

Frank quickly surveyed the lot. "Nothing to stop the crooks once they got the gold this far," he concluded.

"Right," Joe agreed. "But how did they get this far? We'll have to talk to the guards."

"You go ahead," Mr. Hardy said. "I'll carry on my investigation here at the mint and talk to the employees."

"And I'm going to have breakfast," Chet stated.

Frank chuckled. "Your second breakfast, Chet."

"Got to keep my strength up if I'm going to solve this case," the stout boy replied airily.

Frank and Joe dropped Chet at a diner and drove to police headquarters. They identified themselves to the sergeant at the desk.

"You're Fenton Hardy's sons?" the officer asked. "That's good enough for me. Around here, we admire your father's work. Come on! I'll let you speak to the prisoners from the mint. Funny thing about them."

"Funny?" Joe prodded.

"They've got to be guilty," the sergeant said, "but they've taken a polygraph, or lie-detector, test. It says they're telling the truth!"

The three men looked sullen. They were Herb Ponty, Fred Walters, and Mike Nicholson. Ponty did most of the talking.

He admitted they had been on duty the night

the gold had vanished. He himself had been stationed in Armstrong's office at the monitor. "Walters was posted at the outer door to the receiving area. Nicholson guarded the steel door to the gold room."

The Hardys cross-examined the men. Had they left their posts during the night? Had they gone to sleep?

"No, not us," Ponty replied defensively. "It's our job to stay awake. Anyway, it wouldn't have made any difference. A thief trying to get in would have kicked off the alarm system."

"You could have turned off the alarm," Joe asserted. "The control button is on the panel in Mr. Armstrong's office."

"If I had," Ponty argued belligerently, "would I have hung around to be arrested? I'd have left with the thieves."

"Yes," Frank said, "but the gold is gone. Have you three any idea how the crooks pulled off the heist?"

"No, we don't remember seeing anything unusual all night," Ponty declared. "When Mr. Armstrong opened the vault the next morning, the gold wasn't there and we were arrested."

Frank and Joe realized they could not get any more information from the prisoners and headed back to the Wakefield Mint.

"This is the most mysterious case we've ever been on," Joe commented.

"It sure is," Frank agreed. "A consignment of

gold vanishes. The guards say they don't know a thing about it. And a polygraph confirms it."

The boys picked up Chet at the diner as he was drinking his third malted. Then they rode back to the mint, where they told Fenton Hardy and John Armstrong about their talk with the accused men.

"How many people know the combination of the vault door?" Frank asked Armstrong.

"As I told your father, only Director Wadsworth and I. You see—"

A screaming siren cut him off. Red and blue lights flashed on the monitor panel. A moving blur appeared on one TV screen.

Armstrong gasped. "There's a thief in the vault!" he cried.

CHAPTER III

"Deep Six F.H."

JOHN Armstrong rushed into his private elevator. Fenton Hardy and the boys crowded in on his heels. The elevator descended three floors and the doors opened.

The noise of the siren was nearly deafening in the subterranean vault. A guard stood at the door of the gold room, which was wide open. He turned toward Armstrong.

"Unauthorized person inside, sir," he announced. "The door was open and he got in."

"I left it open, Porter," Armstrong confessed. "I thought Millard and Lajinski had nearly finished counting the gold and would close it when they came out. My mistake."

"They hadn't finished when the siren went off," Porter replied.

He led the way inside. The two men in shirt-sleeves were still there, talking to a third, who looked embarrassed.

"I didn't know a laser beam crossed the gold room," he protested. "I got in the way by accident when I came in to see why the door was open."

Frank stared at him. "If you're an employee of the mint, why don't you know about the alarm system in the vault?"

"I'm new here," the man replied sulkily.

Porter nodded. "That's true. We took him on three days ago. He hasn't had time to learn the ropes, but he'll catch on."

Armstrong ordered that the siren be turned off and sent the man to his post; then he escorted his visitors to his office. He sat down in his swivel chair and mopped his brow with a large handkerchief from his breast pocket. Mr. Hardy took a stuffed leather easy chair. The boys occupied a couch.

"Mr. Armstrong," Frank began the conversation, "you were saying that only you and Mr. Wadsworth, the director, know the combination to the steel door of the gold room. Do you think somebody else could have learned it?"

"I suppose someone could in spite of all our precautions," Armstrong admitted. He added, "The gold was shipped from the Swiss Gold Syndicate in Zurich. The bars might be smuggled back there for resale by a shady international financier. I'd better send an agent to Zurich to investigate."

Fenton Hardy smiled. "Two agents," he suggested. "I dare say Frank and Joe will volunteer. They're on their spring vacation."

"Will you, boys?" Armstrong asked eagerly.

The Hardys quickly agreed. Chet looked crestfallen, but said nothing. Armstrong turned to him. "You're included if you want to be."

"Oh, great!" Chet said, and smiled again.

"The place to begin is the Swiss Gold Syndicate," Armstrong pointed out. "They handle transactions on the world-wide gold market, and know about this theft. I'm sure they'll be glad to cooperate. I'll set up an interview for you."

He made a long distance call to Zurich. While he spoke, the expression on his face changed from a frown to utter surprise. When he hung up, he said, "I think we have our first clue!"

"What happened?" Fenton Hardy asked.

"I didn't speak to Johann Jung, the director of the syndicate. He's in South Africa, inspecting gold mines, and won't be back till next Monday. But his assistant just told me that he received a phone call from a man who said that he should watch out for the Wakefield gold. It is expected to be sold in Zurich illegally in about two weeks."

"Wow!" Frank said. "Who was the caller?"

"He didn't identify himself. But I hope you can find out. You're supposed to be in Jung's office Monday at two in the afternoon."

Fenton Hardy arose. "That gives us some time for sleuthing here before you leave," he said. "I have a notion the crooks have already flown the gold out of the Wakefield area or are about to. Transporting it by truck on the highway would be too risky. I'll alert the airlines. You boys check the charter carriers. Also scout around and see if you can find a private airstrip where a plane could take off with a cargo of gold bullion. I'll meet you at the garage later."

The three boys went out and got into the Hardys' car. Frank turned on the ignition and headed toward the center of town. Suddenly he circled around the block and stopped at a phone on the corner.

"Frank, what's up?" Chet asked.

"I think we should check out Mr. Armstrong's story."

Chet's eyes widened in astonishment. *"He* isn't a suspect!"

Joe spoke up. "Frank's right, Chet. Everybody's a suspect in this case."

Frank found Armstrong's address in the phone book and the address of Wakefield's only charter airline. They drove first to the man's house. A motherly woman answered the door.

"Mr. Armstrong is not at home," she told them. "I'm Mrs. Wright, his housekeeper. Mr. Armstrong is a bachelor."

Frank mentioned the night of the gold theft. "Was Mr. Armstrong at home that night?"

"Oh yes. He returned from the mint in time

for dinner, as usual. And he didn't leave the house till the following morning."

Frank thanked the housekeeper and the boys resumed their drive to the center of Wakefield.

"That clears Mr. Armstrong," Frank commented. "He was in bed when the gold vanished from the mint." In a few minutes Frank parked in front of the Carrier Consolidated office on Main Street. The boys went inside. They looked around in surprise. The office was a dusty cubbyhole. A pile of burlap bags lay in one corner, and a half-filled coke bottle stood on the counter. An old plaque on the wall proclaimed that Carrier Consolidated would ferry any cargo anywhere.

"This place could use a cleanup," Frank muttered. "If only Aunt Gertrude were here! She'd give the guy in charge a piece of her mind."

"I'll see if he's in the back room," Joe said. He went around behind the counter. Suddenly a hand pointed a round metal barrel at him through the doorway!

"Watch out!" Chet whispered hoarsely. "He's got a gun."

Before Joe could move, a heavyset individual came through the doorway. "Look here," he said. "This is our newest fire extinguisher. Point it like a pistol, pull the trigger, and presto! It shoots foam all over the blaze. Neat idea, eh?"

"Neat is right," Joe answered. "I thought it was a real pistol."

The man put the fire extinguisher on the shelf behind him. "Carrier Consolidated, at your service," he said.

"Any flights to Zurich, Switzerland?" Frank asked.

"Sure. What's on your mind?"

"We're working on a deal involving a shipment," Frank said.

The man reached for a ledger. "We had two flights to Zurich this month: a cargo of tin and a lumber shipment. The next flight will be in approximately a week. What's the weight going to be?"

"Uh—about two hundred pounds."

"No problem."

"Okay. We'll let you know when the deal goes through," Frank said, and thanked the man for the information.

As the boys were leaving the office, they almost ran into a woman who came through the door and walked up to the counter. She was the waitress from the Stacy Hotel!

Frank nudged Joe as he started to close the door behind him. "What do you know about that?" he whispered.

"Let's see if we can hear any of their conversation," Joe replied and left the door open a crack.

The three friends stood still and pressed their ears against the door, but there was only the sound of muffled voices.

"What now?" Chet asked. "This is strange."

"Let's go to the Stacy and check up on the waitress," Frank suggested. "Maybe she had a reason for being nosey last night."

They went to the hotel and spoke to the manager. "We'd like to talk to your pretty, red-haired waitress," Frank began. "Is she in?"

"No, it's her day off," the man replied with a grin. "But there's no use in trying to date her."

"Oh?" said Frank.

"Sure. Her husband runs the Carrier Consolidated office. He'd give you a hard time."

The boys wanted to roar with laughter, but instead pretended to be embarrassed and left quickly.

"What do you know!" Frank said when the boys were back in the car.

"That you're some smoothy," Chet needled him.

Joe was serious. "Maybe both the husband and the wife are involved in our case."

"What do we do now?" Chet asked.

Frank started the engine. "Let's see if we can find a private airstrip."

The superhighway curved around Wakefield to the north, east, and south. An undeveloped area lay to the west. They decided to scout in that direction. Frank parked at a dead end, and the boys crossed a field on foot. Then they plunged into the woods.

For two hours they tramped between groves of trees and thick bushes. They stumbled over stones and fallen tree trunks. Brambles tore at their clothing and scratched their hands. Doggedly they puffed up hills and down into ravines.

Finally Chet halted and sat down on a boulder, perspiration streaming down his face. His breath came in great gasps. He held up a hand and let it fall limply into his lap. "Fellows, I've had it!" he announced.

Joe grinned. "Don't give up now, Chet! You're getting rid of that spare tire around your middle. Besides, you've got to walk back out of the woods."

Chet groaned. "Don't remind me."

Frank was surveying the ground beyond the boulder. Suddenly he called to the others. Joe raced over. Chet followed slowly.

"What's up?" Joe asked eagerly.

"Tire marks on the ground!" Frank exclaimed. "A car went right through the woods!"

"It probably came from the dirt road we crossed a couple of miles back," Joe theorized. "Where did it go?"

"Let's find out," Frank urged.

Trained woodsmen, the boys followed the tire marks. They noted how the dried-out, brown grass was flattened, and how the vehicle had run over bushes and around trees. Silently the three sleuths pursued the trail through a thicket to where the woods ended. All the trees and shrubs had recently been cleared away in the shape of an oblong.

"It's an airstrip," Frank said in a low voice. "Do either of you see a plane?"

"No," Chet answered, and Joe shook his head. They scouted around the airstrip in Indian file, with Frank in the lead. They had nearly returned to their starting point when Joe noticed sunlight gleaming on metal in a grove of trees.

"I'll investigate," he offered. Dropping to the ground, he crawled to a large bush, peered through the bare branches, and saw a car parked in the grove. Nobody was in sight, so he waved to his companions to follow him.

The car was old and battered. Scratches on the fenders showed it had been driven a long distance through the woods. It had no license plates.

Finding the doors unlocked, Joe opened the glove compartment and took out a sheet of paper lying inside. Frank and Chet peered over his shoulder as he read a short typewritten message.

DEEP SIX F.H.

CHAPTER IV

Stop Thief!

THE boys were shocked. Frank felt cold chills run up and down his spine.

"I'll bet F.H. stands for Fenton Hardy!" he exclaimed.

"And deep six means get rid of him," Joe added grimly.

"No wonder your dad said it was a dangerous case," Chet put in. "We'd better let him know the gang's after him."

They marched back to the dirt road and on to their car. Joe drove to the garage, where Mr. Hardy was already waiting. Frank quickly explained to him about the airstrip near the Wakefield Mint and the car hidden in the clump of trees.

"Here's what I found in the glove compartment," Joe said, handing him the message.

Mr. Hardy read it thoughtfully. "This ties in

with that phone call I received," he said. "Whoever stole the gold wants me off the case. When he realized that his warning had no effect, he and his pals decided to use other measures."

"What now, Mr. Hardy?" Chet asked.

"Leave the car where it is. Don't let on to anyone that you've seen it. I'll keep the area under surveillance and see who comes back to the spot. That might break the case wide open. I only hope," he added wryly, "that the person who is to receive this message has not seen it yet!"

Franked looked doubtful. "I think Joe and I shouldn't go to Zurich, Dad. It's too dangerous for you to be here without us."

Joe supported his brother. "We'll stay in Wakefield and help you out in case of trouble."

Fenton Hardy shook his head. "I realize the danger," he confessed. "But I'll watch my step, and take my assistant, Sam Radley, off his case to give me a hand if necessary. We must look into the Zurich angle, and my sons are naturals for the assignment. Chet, if your folks consent to your going, too, I'm sure Frank and Joe will be glad to have you along. Go home to Bayport and arrange for your flight."

Reluctantly the boys drove away early the next morning. On the way Chet begged to stop in New York to see the gold exhibit at the Early Art Museum before returning to Bayport.

The Hardys consented and they went on to

New York City. Joe spotted a parking lot only a few blocks from the museum. They left the car and walked to the building. A large sign over the entrance read: SCYTHIAN GOLD. The words below stated that the art objects had been sent to the United States by the Soviet Union under a cultural-exchange program.

Chet assumed a learned expression. "The Scythians lived in an area that now belongs to Russia," he intoned. "That's why the Russians have the Scythian gold. They dug up a lot of it in places where those guys camped."

Frank smiled. "Very interesting, Chet. We'll hear the rest of your lecture later, Professor Morton."

The boys were the first viewers to arrive at the museum. The man in charge of the exhibition was a Russian with jet-black hair and a black spade-shaped beard. He wore black clothes and a ring with a large black stone, which gleamed as he gestured.

"I am Ivan Orlov," he introduced himself. "Perhaps you would care to have me describe our Scythian gold."

Chet waved a hand. "That won't be necessary," he declared. "I'm a pro when it comes to gold."

Frank nudged Joe. He concealed his mouth with his hand and whispered, "Chet's up to his old tricks, telling the experts he knows more about their subject than they do."

Joe grinned. "Let's see if he gets away with it this time."

Orlov gave Chet a dubious look. "I do not doubt you, my friend," the Russian said, "but surely—"

"I'm an adept in golden artifacts," Chet told him. "And I've got a diploma to prove it."

"I have never heard of such a title," Orlov said coolly. "But please go inside." His black ring reflected rays of light as he gestured toward the first room of the exhibition.

The boys entered, noticing a sign with the words ANIMAL CHAMBER. Large locked cases held gleaming gold figures of horses, dogs, bulls, deer, mountain goats, tigers, and many other species.

"Those Scythians were big on animals," Chet observed. "They made gold representations of everything that moved."

The Bayporters walked through the display, marveling at the high quality of the Scythian art. They stopped before a huge vase ornamented in gold with the figure of a tiger leaping toward the horns of a defiant bull.

"Siberian tiger," Chet identified the big cat.

The next case contained nothing but replicas of horses, large and small, reclining and standing, jumping and galloping.

"Don't tell me, Chet," Joe said. "Let me guess. The Scythians rode a lot."

"Right. They were terrific riders."

A small figurine in the lower left-hand corner caught their interest. It was a golden horse, rearing on its hind legs. The animal was perfectly modeled with uplifted head and tossing mane.

"I'd like to own that one," Joe remarked. "I'll bet Mother would put it on the mantel in our living room."

Frank grinned. "Aunt Gertrude would surely keep it polished," he added.

While they sauntered around the Animal Chamber another visitor came in and looked at the display with intense interest. He was a middle-aged man with gray hair, dressed in a pin-striped suit. Under his right arm he clutched a leather briefcase, his hand tightly grasping the handle as if he were afraid somebody might snatch it from him.

As the stranger stepped back to get a better view of the figurine of the rearing horse, he bumped into Joe. The briefcase fell to the floor. The man instantly reached down and picked it up.

"Excuse me," he apologized in a high-pitched voice tinged with a slight Spanish accent. "I did not see you."

"No harm done," Joe said cheerfully.

The boys went into the next room, the Ornament Chamber. Every case gleamed with rows of Scythian rings, necklaces, bracelets, pins, brooches, earrings, buckles, and other items of personal adornment.

In an authoritarian voice Chet told his friends about the dress of the ancient tribe. "The Scythian girls went in for gold in a big way," he said, "and the men, too. Everybody wore—"

He was interrupted by a frenzied shout from the Animal Chamber. "Stop, thief!"

Alarmed, the boys hurried out into the hallway. At the far end they saw the stranger with the briefcase and the Spanish accent push through the revolving door. A guard dashed from the Animal Chamber and ran after him. The three Bayporters joined the chase.

When they reached the street, however, the fugitive had already hailed a taxi and was speeding away in the traffic.

"What luck!" Frank fumed. "And there isn't another cab in sight."

"Mr. Orlov will be furious," the guard said, his voice trembling with fear. "But I noticed it too late—"

"Exactly what happened?" Frank asked.

"That man ran out of the Animal Chamber. I became suspicious and checked. I found that the glass in one of the display cases had been cut open. A figurine was missing. I alerted Orlov and took off after the thief."

"Was anyone else in the room at the time?" Frank queried.

"No. Mr. Orlov had gone to his office. Oh, just before the robbery a tall blond man came out of the room and buried his cigarette butt in the bucket of sand in the hallway. I appreciated that because we don't want a fire in the museum. The man went upstairs. In a moment the thief appeared. Obviously he waited until he was alone in the room, then stole the figurine."

The boys found Orlov in the Animal Chamber in front of a display case. A piece of glass had been cut out neatly, and the figurine of the rearing horse that Frank had admired was missing.

The Russian was extremely agitated. He demanded to know what had become of the thief.

"He got away, Mr. Orlov," the guard replied. "Jumped into a taxi."

Orlov began wringing his hands. "Americans! You cannot trust them. I never should have brought the gold here. Our government will be very angry!"

"Maybe we can help you recover the piece," Frank offered. "We have been doing some detective work. Unfortunately, the thief seems to have left no clue."

"I don't know about that," Chet spoke up. "While you were staring after that taxi, I picked this up from the sidewalk. Maybe the guy dropped it!"

He held up a telegram. The others crowded around and read the message.

PEDRO ZEMOG. TAKE CONSIGNMENT TO ZURICH. A.P.

CHAPTER V

The Bulging Briefcase

CHET grinned with a self-satisfied expression as the others read the telegram. "The Hardys aren't the only detectives around here." He chortled.

Joe scratched his head. "But what does the message mean?"

"Search me," Chet replied.

Frank turned to the Russian curator. "Mr. Orlov, does the name Pedro Zemog suggest anything to you?"

"Nothing!" Orlov answered. "Nothing!"

"What about A.P.?"

"Nothing."

The Hardys wondered about the briefcase Zemog had been carrying. Had he opened it in the museum and slipped the figurine inside?

"I saw nothing!" Orlov said.

The guard added, "The thief did not open his briefcase when I saw him. As a matter of fact, he acted as if it were made of solid gold, and he held it very tightly."

"Your police had better do something about getting my ancient horse back!" Orlov exclaimed impatiently. "This theft could be a serious matter between our two countries."

"Yes," Frank agreed. "You'll have to report it right away. But perhaps we can help you. Mr. Zemog is headed for Zurich according to this telegram. We're planning to go there ourselves. Mr. Orlov, would you like us to try to find the thief?"

Orlov stared at him. "You—but who *are* you?"

Frank introduced himself, Joe, and Chet and told Orlov about his father's work.

The Russian became interested. "You are going to Zurich? Good. I will let you pursue the case in Switzerland."

Joe had a sudden thought. "What about the tall blond man? If he's still upstairs, he might be able to tell us something about the thief."

Orlov gave the boys permission to search the building. They rushed upstairs, but could not find anyone who fitted the blond man's description. They returned and reported their failure.

"He must have left by this time," Orlov said. "Too bad we did not think of looking for him sooner."

"Maybe the guy didn't know anything was wrong and simply strolled out after he looked at the exhibition," the guard added.

Frank and Joe promised Orlov they would stay on the case. Then they went with Chet to the parking lot.

"Let's stop at police headquarters," Frank suggested. "We may be able to explain the loss of the gold horse better than Mr. Orlov."

He took the wheel and a few minutes later they were talking to the lieutenant on duty. He agreed to cooperate. Hearing their names, he asked if Frank and Joe were the sons of Fenton Hardy. When he learned that they were, he said, "Fenton is a great detective. I'm glad to hear you're following in his footsteps."

After the lieutenant heard the description of the suspect, he shrugged his shoulders. "Middle-aged man with gray hair, pin-striped suit, carrying a briefcase. Hundreds of men in New York match that description. But I'll put out a bulletin on him and alert the airlines. Who knows? We might be lucky."

The boys thanked the lieutenant and drove to Bayport. After dropping Chet at his house, the Hardys hurried home.

They found their mother in the living room, reading a magazine. She was a pleasant woman who worried about the cases her husband and her sons handled. But she had confidence in them and knew that they had squeezed out of tight situations many times.

"Frank, Joe," she greeted them. The boys

hugged her. "I'm relieved to see you. What have you been doing?"

"Pretending we're gold bugs," Joe said with a chuckle.

Another voice interrupted. "Bugs? We don't want any bugs in this house! What are you boys up to now?"

The speaker was their aunt Gertrude, Fenton Hardy's sister, who lived with the family. She was often stern with her nephews, but they knew she was very fond of them. Miss Hardy admired their skill in solving mysteries, although she tried not to show it.

Joe laughed. "Aunt Gertrude, these aren't the kinds of bugs you sweep out the back door with your broom."

"We're not talking about entomology, the science of bugs," Frank added with a grin.

"Goldology would be more like it," Joe quipped.

Gertrude Hardy sniffed. "You boys can keep your ologies and your bugs," she stated firmly. "Now explain your explanation."

"Dad's trying to recover a shipment of gold that was stolen from the Wakefield Mint," Frank told her, "and we're helping him. As a matter of fact, we'll be going to Zurich, Switzerland, as soon as we can get a flight."

"Isn't that a risky adventure?" his mother asked.

Frank reassured her. "We'll interview the director of the Swiss Gold Syndicate and ask if the gold has been routed through there."

"You might get buried by an avalanche," Aunt Gertrude remarked. "What will you do then?"

"We'll wait for a Saint Bernard dog to find us," Joe needled his aunt. "Seriously, though, we'll be all right."

"We don't want to stay away too long," Frank said. "Not when we have your delicious pies to come back to."

Gertrude Hardy smiled and smoothed back her hair. She could never resist a compliment about her cooking, and promptly invited her nephews into the kitchen for cherry pie and homemade whipped cream.

The next morning Chet phoned. He was glum. "Dad says I have to stay home and help on the farm," he reported. "Have fun, fellows, and round up the gold heisters."

Frank and Joe flew out of Kennedy Airport the following evening. They would have liked to stay in the city longer to see if they could trace Pedro Zemog, but could not book a later flight that would get them to Zurich in time for their appointment with Johann Jung.

Their jet zoomed up from the runway, climbed into the sky, and circled over New York's skyscrapers. Frank and Joe settled near the rear and got a good view of the Empire State Building, the towers of the trade center, and the tip of lower Manhattan. Soon the plane gained altitude and all they could see below them were puffy white clouds.

"I wonder if there's a connection between the Wakefield gold and the Scythian treasure," Frank said thoughtfully.

"Could be," Joe replied. "Both came from the Soviet Union."

"And it's our job to find both," Frank reminded his brother. "The consignment mentioned in the telegram Zemog dropped—could it be gold bars that vanished from Wakefield?"

"Good question," Joe replied. "Maybe we'll find the answer in Zurich."

He slipped out of his seat into the aisle and went for a drink of water near the center of the plane. Then he strolled up front and finally started back. He noticed a man with gray hair, dressed in a dark brown suit. Though he was asleep, he guarded a briefcase under one arm.

Joe paused a moment. "That guy resembles the thief from the museum, Pedro Zemog," he thought. "Too bad he's asleep. I wish I could find out if he speaks with a Spanish accent."

Joe went to ask a stewardess. She replied that the man had not spoken so she did not know.

Joe returned to his seat and informed Frank of his suspicion. Frank immediately made a trip to the front of the plane. On his way back he glanced at the man, who was still sleeping.

"That guy resembles the thief from the museum!" Joe
thought.

When Frank returned, Joe asked, "What do you think?"

"Hard to tell. We're looking for a guy with a Spanish accent. Let's wait till he wakes up. If this passenger is not Zemog, we could get into real big trouble by accusing him of being a thief."

"But didn't you see the bulge in his briefcase?" Joe asked. "It could be the gold horse."

"Joe, the man had to go through the detection center at the airport. A gold object would have been spotted and he would have been arrested."

"That's right," Joe had to admit.

"We'd better sit tight until we get to Zurich," Frank urged, "unless we hear him talk in the plane."

The stewardess arrived with a late dinner, which the boys lost no time in eating. After that, they checked on the suspect again. He had obviously not eaten and was still sleeping.

The boys returned to their places, pushed the reclining seat as far back as they could, and slept as the jet thundered toward Europe. When the Hardys awoke, they saw a magnificent view through the window. Snow-covered mountains spread far and wide beneath their plane. Tall peaks towered toward the sky. Villages nestled in the valleys.

"We're over the Alps!" Joe exclaimed.

Frank glanced at his watch. "By my reckoning, we're over Switzerland already."

Over the loudspeaker a stewardess advised passengers to fasten their seat belts. The jet hissed over Lake Zurich, which extended from the city to the high mountains. The pilot kept on course and came down for a perfect landing at the airport. He taxied to the terminal, braked to a stop, and shut off the engines.

Frank and Joe stood up and tried to reach the suspect, but passengers blocked the aisle. The man in the brown suit waited at the head of the line to debark. Within minutes, he was off the plane.

Watching him through the window, the Hardys saw him hasten to the terminal and into the building. Finally Frank and Joe arrived too. By the time they passed through customs, their quarry was headed toward the exit with long, swift strides. Lugging their suitcases, the Hardys pursued him as fast as they could. They caught up with him at the taxi rank.

He whirled and glared at them when Frank spoke to him. "We're interested in what happened in New York," the boy said.

An expression of fear came over the man's face. Suddenly he hurled himself at Joe, bowling him over backwards. Joe collided violently with Frank. The impact caused both the Hardys to lose their footing. They fell to the pavement in a heap.

A taxi bore down on them at full speed!

CHAPTER VI

Over the Cliff!

INSTINCTIVELY resorting to judo, Joe rolled to the right of the speeding taxi. Frank did a somersault to the left.

The vehicle careened between them and jolted to a halt. *"Was ist los?"* the driver shouted at them. *"Was machen Sie denn da?"*

The Hardys scrambled to their feet. Frank tried to apologize in his high school German: *"Entschuldigen Sie bitte."*

The driver responded with a tirade in German before going on to pick up a fare.

Frank straightened his jacket. "Joe, I think he was telling us off for scaring him. What happened to Zemog?"

"He's gone!" Joe said glumly, looking at the passengers lining up for taxis. "He must have disappeared while we were nearly getting run over by that cab."

They walked to the end of the line and finally

got an empty taxi. Frank told the driver to take them to the William Tell Hotel. At the desk, they signed identification cards and received a room key. They set their luggage inside and tidied up their appearance, then went to the Zurich police headquarters.

Frank explained to an English-speaking captain named Hartl that Pedro Zemog, a suspected thief, was somewhere in the city. Joe inquired whether the Swiss authorities had any information about the man.

The officer checked through the files and made a phone call. Then he turned back to the Hardys.

"Pedro Zemog has no criminal record in our country," he informed them. "But we will watch for him. Tell me where you are staying, and we will call you if we learn anything."

"Thank you," Frank said. "We're at the William Tell for the next few days."

The boys returned to their room and unpacked, then contacted the Swiss Gold Syndicate.

Mr. Jung's assistant told them there had been no more anonymous phone calls. "I asked a lot of people around town," he said, "but found out nothing. I doubt anything will transpire over the weekend. Since Mr. Jung is coming back Monday, perhaps the caller will try to get in touch with him personally."

Frank thanked the assistant and hung up. "What do we do now?"

Joe shrugged. "Let's see the town."

Taking the elevator to the lobby, they found people at the registration desk or following porters who carried their luggage. Others inspected items in the souvenir shop and relaxed in comfortable chairs. The Hardys paused to look at postcards on a revolving stand. Joe twirled it.

"Hey," said a young American, "you just took the card I wanted." A youth about Frank's age peered at them from behind the revolving stand.

"Sorry about that," Joe apologized. "I didn't know you were on the other side."

The two boys started a conversation and Frank joined them. The youth said his name was Rory Harper. He was in Switzerland to see the country and do some skiing.

"Listen," Rory said, "I'm here with three girls, my sister Alice, my girl friend Jane Owens, and their friend Karen Temple. They're standing over there by the window. Want to join us for a soda?"

Frank and Joe peered in the direction of the window and broke out in grins after glimpsing three very attractive teen-aged girls.

"Sure, we'll be glad to," Frank said.

After introductions, the Americans sat down at a low table in the lobby and ordered sodas. Rory's group talked about home and their vacation in Switzerland.

Karen set her glass down on the table. "Joe," she said, "do you ski?"

"A little," Joe answered. "So does Frank."

"That's great!" Alice exclaimed. "We're

leaving today. Want to join us for the weekend?"

Frank and Joe looked at each other. "We don't have to be back till Monday morning, Joe," Frank said.

"And there's nothing we can do here in the meantime," Joe added.

"Good. Then it's all settled," Rory said. "We can rent our gear at the lodge. Let's go!"

The young people went to their rooms and quickly packed warm clothing in an overnight bag, then met in front of the hotel. They hailed a large taxi and the driver let them off at the railroad station.

On the way to the nearest ski resort, they watched the beautiful landscape as the train snaked up the mountains. They exchanged cheerful banter.

"I hope you guys are pros," Rory said. "You'll have to move fast to keep up with me."

"That's right," his sister added. "Rory is fast— on his rear end!"

"Aw, Alice, don't say that!"

Jane giggled. "We should modify that statement. Sometimes he's fast on his stomach, too! I'll never forget that time in Vermont when he slid down head first."

"Oh, that was a bad spill I took," Rory admitted. "My hat went one way, my goggles another, the poles almost hit another skier, and if the safety straps hadn't held the skis, they would have arrived at the lodge without me."

"What were you trying to do, wind up in the hospital?" Joe kidded.

"No," Karen said. "He was just trying to imitate Herman the German, who did a somersault over a three-foot mogul."

"He's one of the instructors up there," Jane explained. "Only Rory can't ski nearly as well as he."

When they arrived at their destination, they hitched a ride to the lodge with a friendly farmer, who chugged along the road in a pickup truck. As soon as they got there, they rented skis, boots, and poles.

Rory and the three girls had brought ski clothes. The Hardy boys each bought a pair of warmup pants to wear with their jackets.

Sunlight glistened on the packed snow of the slopes, and skiers looked like moving colored dots on a white sheet.

After the Americans had bought their lift tickets, they lined up for one of the chairs. Joe paired off with Karen, Frank with Alice, and Rory got on the lift with Jane.

"Wait for us when you get up there!" Rory yelled to the first pair.

"Will do," Joe called back as he watched a girl in a red suit expertly parallel down the slope.

When they arrived at the top, they surveyed the mountain. Alpine peaks formed the skyline around them. The snow-clad terrain dropped away at their feet into a steep run. A colorful white sign with an arrow read: AUTOBAHN–EXPERT ONLY.

Frank held up a hand. The rest gathered around him in a circle.

"Have any of you skied this slope before?" he asked.

He received only negative answers.

"Then we'd better take the Mouse Run over there first. That's intermediate," he advised.

Joe and the girls agreed, but Rory shook his head vehemently. "No, that's too easy for me," he said. "I'm going to take the Autobahn and beat you all to the bottom. See you later!"

He gave a strong push with his poles and began to parallel over the lightly packed powder.

"We'd better not let him go alone," Frank called out. "If you girls think you're up to it, let's follow him."

"We'll make it," Jane said.

Frank led the way to the starting point and pushed off with his poles. Joe and the girls followed. The slope took them in a long semicircle and once narrowed to a steep trail, where they had to go in single file. When it widened again, Frank swiftly decreased the gap between himself and Rory and caught up with him about three hundred feet from the bottom.

"Hey, slowpoke!" he yelled as he overtook the other boy.

Rory tried to catch Frank, but hit a slippery spot and fell.

This gave Joe and the girls enough time to pass him, and they waited at the bottom with Frank.

"Did you say you were a pro?" Karen joshed him.

"I hit an icy spot," Rory said lamely. "My luck!"

"No excuses," Jane said and laughed. "Just do better next time."

Rory looked at the Hardys. "You guys ski well," he admitted.

"We go to Vermont quite a bit," Frank said.

They spent an hour or so skiing the Autobahn and surrounding slopes, then they rode up a different lift, which took them to a trail called St. Gotthart's Pass. A barricade blocked the way and a sign read: DANGEROUS SNOW CONDITIONS. TRAIL CLOSED.

"We don't want to ski down there," Frank observed. "Let's go to the right and get another run."

"Aw, that sign doesn't mean a thing," Rory said flatly. "I'm not afraid to ski down there. According to the map, this connects with a slope called Rim Run, which sounds interesting. Let's go anyway!"

He quickly slipped around the barricade and was halfway through the first turn before Frank could convince him not to go.

"Girls," Frank said, "Take another run. We'll meet you at the bottom."

"Okay," Jane said. "But be careful."

Joe followed his brother, who was having trouble on the slippery surface. "Rory is crazy!" he fumed. "He's going to kill himself and us along with him by going down this death trap!"

Uneven and rocky under the snow, the trail was narrow, the ridges precipitous, and the gorges deep.

"This is like Russian roulette," Frank muttered to himself. "Guess wrong, and it's your last chance. It's over the edge, and somebody else picks up the pieces at the foot of the cliff!"

He was relieved when he saw he was catching up with Rory. "I'll head him off," Frank thought.

But Rory seemed determined not to be passed. He skied at top speed along ridges and past gorges. Reaching a steep decline flanked by an icy cliff, he looked back over his shoulder to see how close Frank was.

The gesture caused him to lose his balance. He slipped head over heels on the ice and lay still!

Wondering how badly his friend was hurt, Frank drove himself forward with his ski poles, his eyes on the crumpled form in front of him. His left ski hit a boulder hidden in the snow. His feet shot out from under him and he landed on his back. The momentum carried him into a long slide on the ice. Frantically he tried to stop himself, but it was no use.

Frank Hardy slid over the cliff!

CHAPTER VII

The Confrontation

JOE skidded to a stop near the top of the cliff, where he had seen Frank vanish.

Rory rose and shook his head woozily. "What happened?"

Joe did not explain. "Go get the ski patrol, pronto!" he yelled.

Rory realized the seriousness of the situation instantly and quickly fixed his skis. Then he schussed down the treacherous trail as fast as he could.

Joe, meanwhile, had taken off his skis and edged himself over the cliff. Frank was clinging by his fingers to a stone ledge about two feet from the top. Beneath him there was a ragged drop.

"Hold on, Frank!" Joe shouted. He climbed onto the ledge. Planting his feet as firmly as he could, he gripped his brother by the arms and struggled to pull him up.

Frank tried to anchor his feet against the cliff, but it was of no use. His skis, dangling on his ankles by the safety straps, clattered on the rock.

"Just hold still," Joe advised. "I sent Rory to get help."

A few minutes later two men from the ski patrol arrived. A rope was dropped over the edge of the cliff, and Joe reached out to catch it. He tied it around Frank, who was drawn to safety by the men above.

"Thanks," Frank said gratefully. "Thanks a lot."

"You should have more sense than to ski down here," one of the men chided. "Don't you realize we close these trails for a good reason?"

"It wasn't Frank's idea." Joe came to his brother's defense. "Rory wanted to get the connection to Rim Run—"

"You can get it another way," the man said curtly. "Now follow us down and don't try it again!"

The boys put their skis back on and made it safely to the intersection of Rim Run. From there it was not far to the bottom, where they met Rory and the girls in the lodge. He was drinking a mug of hot chocolate and was glumly stroking the pigeon's egg on his forehead.

"Boy, do I have a few choice words for you!" Frank said, anger welling up in him again.

"Oh, please don't!" Rory said, rolling his eyes

and pointing to his head. "I've ruined my beauty externally and it doesn't feel so hot internally either!"

The Hardys laughed. "Serves you right, my friend," Joe said. "And I think now we'd better quit!"

The skiers returned their equipment and found an inexpensive guesthouse in which to spend the night. The following day the Hardys skied till early afternoon, then said good-by to their new friends, who planned to stay for a few more days. Frank and Joe took the train back to Zurich.

At the William Tell Hotel, Frank phoned police headquarters and spoke to Captain Hartl.

"We're still looking for Zemog," he informed the boy.

"Any clues?"

"Negative."

After lunch the following day the boys walked to the Swiss Gold Syndicate. It was nearby in a gray limestone building.

"Looks like a fort," Joe commented.

"Sure does," Frank agreed. "It's made of stone and filled with gold."

The brothers identified themselves to one of the guards, who escorted them to the office of the director. It was a large room with a high ceiling, thick rugs on the floor, and small stone-framed windows.

Johann Jung, a tall, dark-haired man, greeted

them in perfect English. "I'm glad you're here," he said. "We've had another call this morning."

"Anonymous again?" Joe asked.

"Yes. It seems that a small time crook has gotten wind of the fact that the Wakefield gold is to be traded on the black market and wants to capitalize on his information."

"What did he say?" Frank asked eagerly.

"He told us to deposit five hundred Swiss *marks* in a small pedestrian tunnel in the old section of town. When he finds the money, he'll leave the information he has."

"Could be a big hoax," Frank said. "He might take the money and run."

Jung nodded. "That's possible," he said. "On the other hand, the Wakefield gold heist is not known to anyone here except myself and the staff. How did he find out about it?"

"Shall we take a chance and pay him, then?" Joe asked.

"I have already," Jung said. "He wanted the money at two o'clock. I sent someone to deposit it."

"Can your man stake out the place and see who our anonymous friend is?" Frank asked.

"I doubt it. The fellow picked an excellent spot for this type of thing. The tunnel is short, narrow, and dark, and many people use it. Anyone waiting inside or on either end would be obvious."

It was not long before there was a knock on the door. A young man entered and handed Jung an envelope. "I deposited the money, sir. This is what I got in return."

Jung took the envelope. "Thank you, Hans. Did you see the man?"

Hans shook his head. "I waited about ten minutes after I left the money before going into the tunnel again. In the meantime, too many people walked through it. I have no idea who took the five hundred *marks* and left this envelope."

"Okay. Thank you."

Hans left and Jung opened the message. It read: "If you want to find out about the Wakefield gold, go to Auerbach's."

"What does that mean?" Frank asked, puzzled.

"Auerbach's is a restaurant in Niederdorf," Jung said. "Maybe you'd better check it out. I'll give you directions."

Half an hour later Frank and Joe walked into Auerbach's. A few people sat at scrubbed wooden tables. The boys approached the elderly man in an apron, who waited on them, and started a conversation in their high school German.

The wrinkle-faced Swiss grinned. "You Americans?" he asked.

Frank nodded. "I'm glad you speak English."

"I lived in Chicago for ten years," the man said.

They found out he was Xaver Auerbach, the owner. After some general comments on Zurich and their travels, Frank said, "We hear people around here trade in gold."

The man looked at him suspiciously. "I don't know what you're talking about."

Joe pulled out a ten dollar bill. "A friend told us to come here if we wanted to buy gold."

Slowly Auerbach took the money. "The only person I hear talking about gold around here is Karl Pfeiffer, and it seems to me he's more talk than action. He usually drops in at five for something to eat."

"Thanks," Frank said. "We'll see him then."

But at five Karl Pfeiffer did not appear. At six there was still no sign of him. Frank slipped Auerbach another bill. "Maybe we could talk to Pfeiffer at his house," he said. "We really can't wait any longer."

"He lives at nine Annastrasse, three blocks from here to your right. The basement apartment."

"Thanks."

The boys found the address and knocked on the door. A sloppy-looking man in his thirties answered.

"Karl Pfeiffer?" Frank asked.

"Ja."

"You speak English?"

"Ja. A little."

"What do you know about the Wakefield gold?"

"Nothing."

"That's not what you've been saying at Auerbach's," Joe put in.

Pfeiffer looked scared. "I don't know what you're talking about. I—"

He looked up as a police car halted in front of the building. Then he whirled around and hurried into his apartment as two officers approached.

"Hey, Pfeiffer, wait!" Frank called out. He ran after the man, who had opened a window on the other side of his living room and was about to climb out.

"Hold it!" Frank said and pulled him back just as the policemen entered the apartment.

"Vielen Dank fuer die Hilfe," one of the officers said, thanking Frank for his help. Obviously they had come to arrest Pfeiffer!

Frank tried to explain why the Hardys wanted to talk to the man, but the policemen spoke little English and the boys' German was not fluent.

"Let's go with them to headquarters," Frank suggested, "and talk to Captain Hartl."

"Right," Joe said. "It'll be interesting to find out why they nailed Pfeiffer."

The officers did not object to the boys' accompanying them to headquarters. When the group arrived, one of them showed Frank and Joe into Captain Hartl's office. They explained what had happened, and the captain looked puzzled.

"Pfeiffer was seen at the scene of a burglary this

morning," he said. "That's why we brought him in. He's a petty thief, but is not known to be a smuggler. Why don't you wait here and I'll talk to him."

The captain was gone for about fifteen minutes. When he returned, he held two envelopes in his hand. "This is a rather amazing turn of events," he said. "Look what we found on Pfeiffer!"

One envelope contained five hundred Swiss *marks,* the other a few gold coins. In the upper left-hand corner of the second envelope were printed the words *Wakefield Mint.*

"Wow!" Frank exclaimed. "What a clue! Pfeiffer is involved in the gold heist!"

"I don't think so," Hartl said. "He told me the whole story. Pfeiffer was approached by a man last week and paid to spread the rumor about the Wakefield gold. The stranger also gave him the envelope with the coins for future use. Then he told him to call the Swiss Gold Syndicate and arrange for them to pay him five hundred *marks* in exchange for the information about Auerbach's."

"Who hired Pfeiffer?" Frank asked.

"He doesn't know. But I know Pfeiffer. He's been in and out of our jail several times. I think he's telling the truth. He was set up by someone who wanted to mislead you!"

"What did the stranger look like?" Joe asked. "Maybe it was Zemog."

"I asked Pfeiffer that," Captain Hartl replied. "The fellow was tall, thin, and in his early thirties. He spoke German without a trace of an accent and Pfeiffer thinks he's either German or Swiss. That doesn't fit Zemog."

"It doesn't," Frank had to admit.

"If I find out anything else about this case and Zemog, I'll contact Mr. Jung," Captain Hartl promised.

"Thank you very much for your help," Frank said and the boys left.

"Let's go back to the hotel and call Jung," Frank said. "I'm sure he'll be glad to hear the police recovered his five hundred *marks*."

A short while later Frank and Joe took the elevator to the fifth floor of the William Tell Hotel. The door clanged open and they stepped into the corridor. At the same time, a man was about to enter the next elevator, which was going down. The boys looked straight at him. He stared in return.

"Pedro Zemog!" Frank exclaimed. Zemog still clutched his briefcase, shielding it with his arm. Then the elevator door closed.

"He's headed for the lobby!" Joe cried. "We may be able to catch him!"

The Hardys took the stairs two at a time. They reached the lobby and looked around. There was no sign of Zemog.

"Too late," Frank groaned.

The desk clerk could not tell them anything about Pedro Zemog, but he did say a man named Jones, who matched their description of Zemog, had been in room 506 and had just checked out of the hotel.

Back on the fifth floor, the Hardys noticed that the door of 506 was open. They went in. The bed was mussed, the drawers half-open, the closet door ajar. A quick tour of the room revealed nothing.

"Zemog didn't leave a single clue," Frank said in disappointment.

"Maybe he did," Joe answered, as he reached into the wastebasket beside a table. He drew out some shredded yellow paper. Carefully he fitted the torn pieces together.

"It's a telegram!" Frank said, looking over his brother's shoulder, as Joe put the last piece in place. The boys felt completely stymied as they read the message:

PEDRO ZEMOG. TAKE CONSIGNMENT TO MEXICO CITY. A.P.

CHAPTER VIII

A Warning

FRANK and Joe stared at each other, wondering again if the telegram referred to the gold stolen from the Wakefield Mint.

Finally Frank shook his head. "It can't be. I think the telegram indicates that the consignment referred to has been in Switzerland and is now to be shipped to Mexico. But the crooks wouldn't be so foolish as to bring the gold to Zurich secretly and then spread a rumor that it would be sold here!"

"I see what you're getting at," Joe agreed. "The rumor was created to keep us far from the place where the Wakefield gold has been, or will be, taken. So Zemog's instructions don't refer to it."

"Right. But let's phone Captain Hartl about the telegram, anyway. We still want to find Zemog for the museum."

Police Captain Hartl promised to alert the airlines about the fugitive's planned trip to Mexico, but said, "Since Zemog called himself Jones at the hotel, he's obviously traveling under an assumed name. That creates a problem. What are your plans?"

"I think we'll go back to Wakefield," Frank said.

"Good idea. If we find Zemog, we will get in touch with the Early Art Museum in New York."

"Thank you very much," Frank said and hung up.

The boys packed and flew home the next morning. When they arrived, their mother greeted them with hugs. "I'm so glad you're back," she said. "I hope you weren't in any danger."

"Well, Frank did a cliff-hanger," Joe said, laughing. He described the skiing party and his brother's accident.

"Why, Frank, you could have been hurt!" Mrs. Hardy exclaimed.

"Mother," Frank assured her, "I knew what I was doing. And anyway, Joe was watching and came to the rescue."

"I wish the two of you wouldn't take such chances." Mrs. Hardy sighed.

"Chances? What chances?" said Aunt Gertrude at the doorway. "Have you boys been up to some of your harebrained stunts again?"

After hearing the story, she shook her head. "You must have nine lives, like they say cats do."

Frank thought, "I used one up on that cliff."

"By the way," Mrs. Hardy put in, "a man named Ivan Orlov phoned and asked for you. I told him you'd be back today. He refused to say what he wanted."

A short while later, the phone rang. Joe answered. The caller was Orlov. "So you are back from Zurich," he said. "Have you brought the Scythian figurine with you?"

Joe confessed that he and Frank had failed to retrieve the golden horse. He described how the boys had spotted Zemog at the Zurich airport and at the William Tell Hotel, and said that the police were looking for him.

"Why did you not have him arrested? Why did you not take the figurine from him?" Orlov demanded.

"We lost him both times."

"Lost him!" Orlov stormed. "You mean you and your brother permitted him to escape?"

"That's about the size of it," Joe said.

"Size? What does that mean—size?"

"It means you're correct, Mr. Orlov."

"You have brought back no clue from Zurich?"

"Yes, as a matter of fact we have," Joe stated. He told the curator about the shredded telegram in Zemog's abandoned hotel room and the message referring to Mexico City.

"You must follow him!" the Russian declared, excited. "You must go to Mexico City at once and find the gold horse! I will pay your expenses!"

Joe informed Orlov that they could not do this until they heard from their father. "He and my brother and I are involved in another case," he explained.

Orlov became angrier. "Another case? What case could be more important than mine? Are you leaving me—how do you say it—in the lurch?"

"Mr. Orlov, if our father can spare us, we'll be glad to pursue your case. But we'll have to check with him first."

"This is too confusing," Orlov complained. "All I can say is that if the gold horse is not restored to me, it will be . . . most unfortunate for your country!"

The Russian hung up so vehemently that Joe felt a painful buzz in his ear.

"Wow! Next time he calls, Frank, you talk to Comrade Orlov!" he said, holding his ear.

"What's up?"

"He's mad at us because we didn't bring his gold horse back from Switzerland. Now he wants us to leave at once and chase Zemog around Mexico City."

The phone rang again. Frank answered it.

"If it's Orlov," Joe muttered, "say I'm off on a moon flight."

This time Fenton Hardy was calling. "I'm in John Armstrong's office and we have you on conference call so we both can hear your report on Zurich," the detective said.

"It was not a success," Frank said and told

about their visit to the Swiss Gold Syndicate, the false lead, and the arrest of Pfeiffer.

Mr. Hardy and John Armstrong agreed that the rumor was undoubtedly a diversionary tactic which the thieves had cunningly used to mislead the Hardys.

Frank told his father about Zemog and the stolen figurine from the Early Art Museum in New York. "Orlov wants us to go to Mexico City," he said. "But we told him that we could only work for him if you don't need us any more."

"Well, I'm up against a stone wall right now," Mr. Hardy said. "Let me talk to John."

The two men conferred for a few minutes, then Mr. Hardy came back on the line. "When you mentioned Mexico City, John remembered something he had been told just the day before the burglary," the detective said. "It had slipped his mind, but now it seems as if it might be a clue!"

"What is it?" Frank asked eagerly.

"One of the guards mentioned that he saw a private plane flying rather low over the mint with the words 'Mexico City' on the fuselage. John paid little attention to it at the time, but now we're beginning to think that perhaps the plane landed on the hidden airstrip here in Wakefield and waited for the gold to be flown out."

"Oh, Dad, that's a great theory!" Frank said, excited.

"The only thing is," Joe put in, "how do you

know Mexico City was the plane's destination?"

"You don't," Mr. Hardy said thoughtfully. Again he conferred with Armstrong for a few minutes, then he said, "John thinks that even if the plane didn't fly to Mexico City, it might have been based there. Since there's nothing for you to do here at this point, he wants you to fly to Mexico and see if you can track down the plane while you're looking for Zemog."

"We'll be glad to check out the Mexican angle," Frank said. "And Orlov will be pleased, too. We'll leave as soon as we can. What's new in Wakefield?"

"No clues," Mr. Hardy replied. "I scouted around the airstrip in the guise of a backpacker and kept the abandoned car under surveillance for three days. No one went near it."

"Was the car stolen?" Frank asked.

"Yes. The owner has it now. By the way, John said if you need any help in Mexico he'll be glad to pay the expenses. He wants that plane tracked down as fast as possible."

"We'll ask Chet, Biff, and Tony to go along," Frank suggested. "This way we can split up and divide the legwork."

"Excellent idea. And good luck!"

Biff Hooper and Tony Prito were two more of the Hardys' close friends. Biff was a husky six-footer who knew how to use his fists. Olive-skinned Tony was a carefree youth who was always ready for an adventure. Like Chet, the two boys had helped Frank and Joe solve some of their mysteries in the past. Frank phoned them at once. "Big doings!" he said. "Make tracks over here in a hurry or get left out!"

Twenty minutes later a series of loud, gunlike reports sounded in the street. Chet's battered jalopy rattled up to the Hardy home, backfiring all the way. Chet was at the wheel, with Biff and Tony beside him. He brought the vehicle to a jolting stop at the curb and turned off the ignition. The jalopy stopped its bucking and subsided.

Tony jumped out and stretched. "Oh, my aching back!" He groaned.

Biff extricated his long legs from under the dashboard. "When you ride with Chet, you hurt all over."

Chet grinned. "How come you guys let me give you a lift if my jalopy scrambles your anatomy?"

"We never learn," Biff said.

The three hurried up the front steps. Frank and Joe were eating large pieces of cherry pie on the porch. "Go right through," Joe told their friends. "Aunt Gertrude is ready for you."

Chet, Biff, and Tony went to the kitchen and reappeared with slices of pie. Tony sat down in a rocking chair, Biff perched on the porch railing, and Chet reclined in a hammock, balancing the loaded plate on his belt buckle.

"Okay," Tony said, "let's have it."

"It had better be good," Biff warned.

"The cherry pie suits me," Chet countered. "But I know what the Hardys are up to."

"What?" Biff demanded.

"Gold!"

"Chet's right," Frank revealed. He briefly told them the story of the Wakefield and Scythian gold. "We are working on both cases," he concluded.

"Next stop—Mexico City," Joe added. "How about you guys joining the expedition, all expenses paid?"

"Wow!" Chet exclaimed, and the other two were equally enthusiastic.

"It might be dangerous," Frank warned.

"We'll outsmart our enemies," Tony vowed.

Chet levered the last piece of pie from his plate into his mouth. He chewed and swallowed with a blissful expression. Then he put out a hand and pushed on the railing, causing the hammock to sway back and forth.

"You fellows can have the crooks," he declared. "I'll stick to archaeology. The Aztecs lived in Mexico City, and had tons of gold. I'd love to see their ancient masks."

Frank shook his head. "You may not have a chance, Chet. Our assignments are the Wakefield gold and the horse figurine Orlov wants back."

Chet gave in. "Well, as long as I get to see

somebody's gold. Aztec or Russian, it's all the same difference."

The others laughed. They were used to their stout friend making jokes when danger lay ahead.

The five spent the rest of the evening planning their expedition. The next morning they drove to the airport and caught a flight to Mexico City. Upon landing, Frank proposed that the group split up and see if they could find the plane from Wakefield.

Chet was to check with the tower, Biff and Tony were to talk to the pilots, and the Hardys would question the mechanics.

Chet went to the tower and discussed the mystery plane with the dispatcher.

"Mexican airlines have many craft marked 'Mexico City,' " the man pointed out.

"This is a private plane," Chet replied. "It flew down from the U.S.A. about a week ago."

The dispatcher checked. "I have no record of the one you describe," he said.

Meanwhile, Biff and Tony had been circulating through the offices of the airlines, questioning pilots. None could tell them anything about an aircraft marked "Mexico City."

Frank and Joe had better luck. The fifth mechanic they interviewed had serviced a private plane with that marking. Its pilot was a young man.

"I heard him mention Palango," the mechanic said.

"Palango?" Joe asked. "What does that mean?"

"I think it's an archaeological term. Better ask Professor Carlos Alvarez at the university. He can tell you all about archaeological digs around here."

"Thanks for the info," Frank said.

He and Joe held a conference near one of the runways. Planes took off and landed, taxiing up to the terminal. Crews removed baggage as lines of passengers alighted.

"It's sure noisy here," Joe said.

They walked to a hangar servicing private planes. A small aircraft stood near them on the runway, ready for takeoff. They could see the pilot checking his instruments.

While they were talking, Chet joined them. Biff and Tony came up at the same time.

"No luck," Chet reported.

"We drew a blank, too," Biff said.

Frank told them not to worry. "We got a clue from one of the mechanics."

"The plane was here, and the pilot mentioned the word Palango," Joe added. "Professor Alvarez at the university might be able to tell us what that means."

"You see?" Chet said triumphantly to Biff and Tony. "The Hardys always get their man. They'll find the gold!"

His words were overheard by the pilot of the small plane near them. He had just climbed out of the cockpit and proved to be a hulking figure in overalls. He carried a long wrench in his right hand.

The man stared at the boys, his brows furrowed. Then he sidled up to them. "What are you guys doing here?" he scowled. "And who are you?"

"Who are *you?*" Biff retorted boldly.

"My name's Murphy, and they don't call me Rumble for nothing. Understand?"

"Understand," Chet said hastily. He was not about to tangle with a man carrying a wrench.

"What are you after?" the pilot demanded.

"Gold," Chet said.

"It has to do with Palango," Joe put in.

Rumble Murphy stepped toward them. Glowering, he slapped the wrench menacingly against the palm of his left hand. "You'd better go home right now if you want to stay healthy!"

CHAPTER IX

Chet's Mistake

RUMBLE Murphy brandished his wrench. Chet stepped back for fear of being hit, but Tony stood still, his hands on his hips. Biff assumed a karate stance.

"That sounds like a threat!" Frank said.

"It *is* a threat!" Murphy snapped.

"What do you mean?" Joe asked.

"You'll find out soon enough if you butt in where you're not wanted."

Joe stepped forward and looked the pilot straight in the eye. "Come on, Murphy!" he demanded. "Why are you threatening us?"

The man's answer was a punch that struck Joe on the jaw. Joe staggered backward and toppled over. Biff and Tony caught him as he fell.

Murphy ran to his plane and jumped in. The boys raced after him. Suddenly Frank shouted, "Hit the ground!"

They all plunged face downward on the runway. A landing plane sped toward them. They felt a gust of air as one wing passed over them with inches to spare! Shakily, the boys got to their feet.

"Lucky you shouted, Frank," Biff said, "or we would have been mowed down."

They watched helplessly as Rumble Murphy took off. He became airborne and vanished into the clouds scudding across the sky.

"Murphy's a real pro when it comes to flying," Frank observed.

Joe rubbed his jaw. "My guess is he's a boxer," he said. "That guy hit me really hard with that haymaker."

The boys walked to the airport terminal.

"We must find out about Palango," Tony remarked.

"Let's set up an appointment with Professor Alvarez," Frank suggested.

Biff clapped Chet on the shoulder. "You're the expert on archaeology, Chet. We elect you to contact the professor."

Chet grinned. "I'll be glad to. Just lead me to the phone."

He made the call to the university. Alvarez said he would welcome the visitors next morning.

The boys claimed their baggage and took a taxi to the hotel at which they had chosen to stay. After freshening up, they decided to use their free time sightseeing.

In the lobby, Frank inquired at the desk about a guide, and soon a wiry Mexican with wavy black hair appeared.

"You want to see Me-hee-co?" he asked the travelers with a friendly grin. "My name is Juan and my car is outside. It will cost you only a few pesos."

They made a deal with the guide, who led them to an old auto with crumpled fenders and a crack in the windshield.

"This must be fifty years old," Joe presumed. His companions were thinking the same thing. Feeling somewhat dubious about its reliability, they climbed in.

Juan started the engine, which wheezed and then made a put-putting sound that seemed about to choke off at any moment. He released the brake and chugged away from the hotel, dispensing tourist information as they rattled along.

First he took them through Mexico City's main square. "The *Zocalo*," he informed his passengers. "Our great plaza."

The area was dominated by the cathedral. They saw the national palace, the library, the School of Fine Arts, and other public buildings in and around the plaza.

Traffic whizzed every which way. Their guide stepped on the gas and headed into it. His passengers braced themselves as he raced ahead of one car and braked sharply to avoid another.

"Chet, this is worse than your jalopy!" Biff muttered out of the corner of his mouth.

They reached a beautiful broad boulevard. The car bumped along past trees, office buildings, crowds of pedestrians, and benches where tourists and citizens relaxed. Next came the markets of Mexico City, colorful areas with shops and outdoor stalls. Most of the vendors were selling fruits and vegetables.

In the Merced Market, Chet tapped the driver on the shoulder and told him to stop. Juan pulled into a side street.

"What's up, Chet?" Frank asked.

"Come on. I'll show you."

They got out and followed him as he walked to a stall with succulent Mexican dishes. The aroma of tacos, tortillas, enchiladas, and chili filled their nostrils. Chet closed his eyes and inhaled rapturously.

"We might have known," Joe said with a chuckle. "Chet never passes up any chow."

"I'm with him this time," Frank said.

The rest echoed the sentiment. They ordered a tortilla for each, including the driver, then strolled around the market, examining stall after stall. Juan talked to them animatedly, and occasionally conversed with the merchants in Spanish.

Chet, Biff, and Tony paused to look at some prints of Mexico City. Frank and Joe wandered down a side street into a dingy alley.

"*Señores,* permit me to tell your fortune!" The speaker was an old woman with piercing black eyes and a black lace veil over her hair. Her shop had an astrological chart of the heavens on the open door. "*Señores,* only a few pesos!" she urged them.

They went in and found her shelves covered with curios—herbs to be distilled for poisons, signs of the zodiac, and dolls with pins stuck in them.

The woman grabbed Joe's hand and began to read his palm. "You have had a recent misfortune," she said in a singsong voice.

Joe rubbed his jaw, which was still sore from Rumble Murphy's punch. "Right," he replied.

Frank extended his hand. "How about reading my future?" he suggested.

The woman surveyed his palm. Her eyes narrowed. "What do I see here?"

"That's what I want to know," Frank said.

"Much gold!"

The Hardys were startled. They tried to query the woman. Finding she would say no more, they paid her and left the shop.

"Could she know about the gold we're after?" Joe wondered.

"Anything's possible," was Frank's opinion.

The Mexican guide continued the sightseeing tour by driving to Chapultepec Park, a broad green area of woods and a lagoon, where entire families were enjoying the outdoors. Children played amid multicolored shrubs, bushes, and flowers. Fountains spouted water.

"Chapultepec," the guide said. "That word means 'grasshopper' in the Aztec language."

His battered car huffed and puffed as he pointed it up the hill. At the top he parked in the grounds of Chapultepec Castle, a white stone building with rounded arches and a tall oblong tower. A piece of sculpture on the terrace represented a huge grasshopper.

Inside, the visitors were streaming through the various halls. The boys from Bayport joined them. They saw costumes worn in Mexico City since Aztec times and the apartment once occupied by Emperor Maximilian, who ruled Mexico during the American Civil War.

"What happened to Emperor Max?" Joe asked.

"We shot him," Juan said laconically.

They climbed up to the roof garden for a view of Chapultepec Park. Frank turned his head. A man with gray hair, wearing a dark suit, was on the other side of the garden. He held a briefcase! Frank tapped Joe on the shoulder and pointed.

"Zemog!" Joe gasped.

The brothers pushed through the crowd, turning and twisting in the press of bodies. At one point they were stopped by a solid wall of visitors and had to detour around them. Struggling and panting, they inched forward. At last they got to the other side.

"I see much gold!" the woman said.

The suspect was gone!

Frank and Joe hurried through the rest of the castle, only to draw a blank in every hall. They ran out to the terrace. Zemog was not there either.

"This is getting ridiculous," Joe fumed. "Zemog pops up in the craziest places, and when we follow him, he dissolves into thin air!"

"We let him escape again, as Orlov would put it," Frank agreed. "Which isn't saying much for us!"

"I'm beginning to think it's Zemog's ghost who's giving us this problem." Joe chuckled.

The boys strolled around the terrace until they found Juan and their friends.

"What happened?" Biff asked. "You took off so fast we didn't even have a chance to offer our help!"

"We think we saw Zemog again," Frank explained. "And as usual, he escaped."

"What do we do now?" Chet asked.

"I think we should finish our sightseeing tour at police headquarters," Joe suggested.

Everyone agreed, and Juan took them to their destination. The boys thanked him for the tour, paid him, and went inside.

The sergeant at the desk spoke English well and listened to their problem with interest. He checked his records for Zemog, but found nothing.

"Zemog is not a Mexican name," the sergeant said. "Unless he uses an alias, we should be able to track him down without too much difficulty. I will check all the hotels and see what I can learn."

The boys returned to their hotel for the night. After breakfast the next morning, they taxied to the university to meet Carlos Alvarez. The professor's office was lined with rows of books on archaeology.

He identified Palango at once. "It is an archaeological site not far from the great ruins of Chichén Itzá on the peninsula of Yucatán. Palango was recently discovered and digging has just begun. It lies in the same area as a lost pyramid of the Mayas. Fifty years ago a hunter reported seeing the pyramid. But since then, every attempt to find it has failed. What is your interest in Palango?"

Frank said that somebody might have flown gold from Mexico City to Palango.

Alvarez was puzzled. "I don't know why anyone would do that. Usually it is the other way around."

He gave them a little lecture on gold, noting that the Aztecs molded it into fine art pieces. "Their artifacts are so good many people cannot tell the difference between Aztec and Scythian."

Chet puffed out his chest. "Oh, I can always tell Aztec stuff!" he boasted.

Alvarez smiled. He took a small piece of gold representing the head of a child from his drawer. "What do you make of that, my friend?"

Chet hefted the gold in his hand. "That's Aztec, all right."

"No, it comes from the Inca civilization down in Peru," Alvarez corrected him.

Chet turned red in the face. His companions snickered, but Alvarez was indulgent. "An easy mistake to make." He soothed Chet's feelings.

That ended the session with the professor. The boys, deciding to run down the Palango angle at once, went to the airport and chartered a plane to fly them to Yucatán.

Three hours later they were on their way. The pilot flew across central Mexico, took the long leg of the journey across the Gulf, and zoomed past the shoreline over the jungle, thick with trees and tropical vegetation.

Suddenly the engine began to sputter. The boys looked at one another in alarm.

"What's happening?" Frank asked tensely.

"I don't know," the pilot replied. "I had everything checked out before we left. But this is definitely trouble."

He worked the controls frantically. But it was of no use. The engine quit and the plane nose-dived toward the jungle!

CHAPTER X

The Boa Constrictor

DOWN, down they plunged! The jungle seemed to be rushing up to meet them and presently they could see the upper branches of the trees!

The pilot fought desperately to bring his plane out of its nose-dive. At the last moment, the engine came to life, and he regained control. They swooped down, then climbed just above the trees. Now he was able to zoom back to a safe altitude.

The pilot mopped his brow. "I don't understand what happened. I double-checked everything before we left Mexico City."

"Could be somebody doesn't want us to get to Palango," Frank observed in a shaky voice.

The plane flew across Yucatán and came down for a landing at Mérida, the main city in the northern Mayan region. The boys climbed out. All were shaken by the near crash.

"*T-t-terra firma* for me," Chet stuttered.

"For me, too," Biff added.

"The Mayas had the right idea," Tony said. "They never fooled around with planes."

The Hardys tried to cheer their pals. "We got here, didn't we?" Joe pointed out.

"Better than hacking our way through the jungle," Frank declared.

The pilot inspected his plane. "Somebody tampered with the engine," he said grimly. "I'll have to repair it."

His passengers checked with airport officials to see if anybody had seen a private plane marked "Mexico City." Nobody had, so the boys decided to go right on to Palango. Frank rented a jeep and drove to Chichén Itzá. All of them marveled at the ruins of temples and pyramids that once were the center of the Mayan culture of northern Yucatán. They asked a policeman about Palango.

"Take the dirt road northeast," the man replied, "and then follow the jungle trail. The Palango dig is at the end of it."

The boys set out, with Biff at the wheel of the jeep. The dirt road ended and the jungle trail began. It was so rough and bumpy through the dense tropical vegetation that they felt sore and bruised. Even well-padded Chet complained. "I'm not made to be a rubber ball," he said.

Biff shifted into low gear. "We should have rented a Sherman tank," he grumbled.

Joe laughed. "How about a swamp buggy?"

The jeep jounced over a large bush. An enor-

mous hole loomed directly ahead! Biff stepped on
the brake and the jeep halted at the edge of the
hole with a jerk that nearly sent Chet flying over
the windshield.

Frank pointed to a pile of fresh earth beside the
trail. "Somebody dug that hole recently. I wonder—"

A splintering sound interrupted him. A giant
tree beside the trail began to sway. It toppled
toward the jeep!

Biff reacted instantly. He stepped on the gas,
wrenched the wheel to the left, and scooted into
the jungle undergrowth flanking the trail just
before the tree fell with a crash. The boys ducked
as the branches lashed over the jeep. Then Biff
cut back out onto the trail beyond the hole and
stopped.

He sighed with relief. "Anyone hurt?" he asked.

The others said no, then Frank proposed that
they look around before going on.

The boys walked to the fallen tree. As Chet inspected the tangle of heavy branches, he remarked, "It's lucky we got out from under."

"The tree would have smashed us," Tony
agreed.

"Look at the trunk!" Joe declared.

It had been chopped nearly all the way
through!

"Someone was setting a trap for us!" Tony exclaimed.

Frank nodded. "He dug the hole to make us

stop, cut the tree with an ax till it was barely standing, and then pushed it over to make it topple on us."

Biff clenched his fists. "That means he must still be around here somewhere. I'll take him over the hurdles!"

He ran back up the trail. Frank and Joe took the underbrush on one side, Chet and Tony the other. The boys scouted through the area but found nothing except scuffed footprints near the base of the fallen tree.

"He got away!" Biff lamented.

"We may as well call off our search," Joe said. "It would be like looking for a needle in a haystack, only this haystack is the Yucatán jungle."

An hour later the group bounced into Palango. A Mayan temple had been partially reclaimed, and nearby a deep excavation revealed further work in progress. Several tents had been set up in a cleared area. Four Americans were there along with a dozen Mexicans, descendants of the Mayas, who had been recruited to help with the dig.

The leader of the archaeological expedition came forward to meet them. He was tall and handsome with black wavy hair. "I'm Steve Weiss," he introduced himself. "It's a surprise to see you. Usually visitors don't get this far in the jungle."

Frank explained that he and his companions were trying to find gold.

"We have already found quite a bit!" said a voice behind them.

The boys turned to see a man wearing white shorts and a pith helmet. He had a superior smile on his face, as if to say that he was doing the visitors a favor by speaking to them. He carried a swagger stick, which he slapped against his leather boot.

"I'm Melville Courtney, assistant archaeologist on the dig," he announced. "I'm also a Hawkins man."

"He means Hawkins College," Joe thought.

"We have already found gold, son," Courtney repeated, "and are scarcely in need of your assistance on that score. The Mayas buried the gold. We retrieved it after much exertion and loss of perspiration.

"I'm sure you realize," Courtney continued, "that your help would be superfluous."

"A job is not what we have in mind," Frank told him.

"Do you have armadillos in mind?" asked a woman who had just walked up. She was short, had golden hair, and a heart-shaped face. She wore a denim shirt and slacks.

"Rose Renda, our biologist," Steve Weiss introduced her. "She just joined us a few days ago."

"I'm an armadillo freak," Rose declared.

Chet scratched his head and gave her a blank look. "Armadillo freak?"

"As you no doubt know," Rose explained, "an armadillo is an armored animal native to these parts. It's about five feet long from snout to tail in the biggest species. The armor on its back is approximately three feet long. The problem I'm researching is this: how is the armadillo related to the glyptodon?"

Now Tony looked blank. "What's a glyptodon?"

Rose smiled. "You mean, what was a glyptodon? It lived millions of years before the armadillo, was about nine feet long, and had five feet of armor. The armor was completely smooth, and had a number of hinges that permitted it to turn more easily."

"And you want to find out how the glyptodon evolved into the armadillo?" Tony asked.

"Yes," Rose replied.

A man carrying a rifle joined the party. He was over six feet tall, slim, and quiet.

"This is Frank Pendleton," Rose said, "our jungle guide. He knows everything about this area."

"I should after twenty years," Pendleton said, smiling.

"I take it you hunt, too?" Tony said with a glance at the man's rifle.

"No. The gun is strictly for self-defense against the dangerous animals of Yucatán and the jungles south of Brazil. I've seen them all."

"You mean jaguars?" Biff asked.

"That, and big snakes—boa constrictors, for instance."

Chet grimaced. "I hope I don't meet one."

"You never can tell what you may meet in the jungle," the guide responded. "I—"

"Time for chow," Weiss interrupted.

Melville Courtney slapped his swagger stick against his boot again. "Dinner is indeed served, such as it is," he said in his high-pitched voice. "K rations and coffee. Really!"

"However you say it," Weiss laughed, "we're all ready to eat." He invited the Bayporters to share their fare, and they sat in a circle on the ground.

After a while Frank asked, "Has anybody here seen a private plane marked 'Mexico City'? We're trying to find it."

No one had.

Joe put the next question to the group. "Have you ever met a man named Pedro Zemog?"

Again, everyone said no.

"Rumble Murphy?"

As the men shook their heads, Rose said, "Why are you looking for these people?"

"Because we're trying to solve the mystery of a gold theft," Joe replied. He told the group about the Wakefield heist and the theft of the ancient horse from the Scythian collection.

Courtney coughed. "Mr. Zemog and Mr. Murphy are obviously not gentlemen," he stated. "I would not care to associate with them."

"But they're part of our mystery," Joe pointed out.

"I don't think you'll solve your mystery here,"

Weiss said. "There's no reason for these gold thieves to bring their loot down here. They'd stick to Mexico City."

Rose lowered her coffee cup. "It looks as if you boys have come a long way for nothing."

Chet grinned. "Not me. I want to look at the Mayan gold you found, because I'm adept in gold artifacts."

"What in the world is that?" Rose asked.

Chet explained his correspondence-course diploma.

Courtney gave him a supercilious look. "That is not like a degree from Hawkins," he stated.

Chet looked hurt.

"Well, it's an interesting title," Steve Weiss interjected to make Chet feel better. "Sure, you can see our gold. The Mayas buried it to keep the Spaniards from getting it. Palango was once a thriving Mayan city. It was subordinate to Chichén Itzá, which you passed through to get here. You must have seen the temple-pyramid there."

"Yes, we did," Frank said.

"Well," the archaeologist continued, "Chichén Itzá also had its Temple of the Warriors, its Court of the Thousand Columns, and its Observatory."

"Observatory?" Tony asked. "Did those people study astronomy?"

"Oh, sure, and in a big way. They kept records of the stars and planets so they could be sure their

Mayan calendar was accurate. They needed to know which days of the year to hold their religious festivals and other ceremonies."

"Palango was minor compared to Chichén Itzá," Pendleton put in. "But it did have a pyramid—the lost pyramid."

"Boy, how can you lose a pyramid?" Biff quipped. "Kind of careless."

Rose laughed. "The fact is that jungle growth covers everything in a few years."

Weiss nodded. "And the jungle's had almost five hundred years to cover the pyramid. When the trees, moss, vines, and creepers have done their work, you can walk within yards of a Mayan building and never spot it."

Pendleton continued. "We know the lost pyramid is about twenty miles from here because a hunter spotted it fifty years ago. But he didn't give the location. Even if we knew that, it would be very hard to hack our way through the jungle. There's the vegetation, the heat, and the insects. As things are, every attempt to find the pyramid has failed because it's like looking for a minnow in the Gulf of Mexico."

"We may never discover it," Rose added, "but we expect to run into a lot of armadillos. The jungle here must be loaded with them."

"It is," Pendleton assured her. "We'll go out after armadillo tomorrow. Like to go along with us, fellows? You can help capture one."

Biff spoke for them all. "That would be great!"

Weiss dug into the camp stores for more tents. Frank and Joe pitched the one they would share on the edge of the clearing near the Mayan temple. Branches of large trees, which surrounded the ancient building, were festooned with trailing moss, giving the scene an eerie look.

The Hardys said good night to their friends and were sound asleep when they were awakened by a terrified shout from Biff's tent. It woke up others in the camp and brought footsteps pounding in his direction.

Joe snapped on his pocket flashlight and opened the flap of his friend's shelter.

"Biff, what's wrong?" he asked.

"On the ground!" Biff cried.

Joe trained the beam of his light lower. A long sinuous form was coiled just inside the door of Biff's tent. The reptile raised its head in a menacing stare and started to hiss.

"It's a boa constrictor!" Chet bellowed. "That thing will squeeze him to death!"

CHAPTER XI

A Mysterious Shot

BIFF crouched at the rear of his tent and eyed the big snake apprehensively. His friends formed a semicircle at the open flap of the canvas, not daring to get too close. The boa constrictor flicked its tongue menacingly.

"What'll we do?" Chet wailed.

"Step aside!" a woman ordered. Rose Renda walked into the tent. She was carrying a large burlap bag, the mouth of which she opened by releasing a draw-string. Just then three Mexican workmen, alerted by Pendleton because of their experience in handling snakes, joined the group.

The jungle guide teased the boa constrictor with a stick until it struck ferociously. As its head hit the ground, Pendleton's hand flashed out and closed on the neck just behind the head.

Two of the other men grabbed the reptile around the body, while the third seized the lashing tail. The four lifted the boa off the ground and dropped it, tail first, into the open burlap bag that Rose was holding. Then they crammed in the sinuous body, and finally Pendleton shoved the head, instantly pulling his hand away. Rose drew the mouth of the bag taut.

"This will make a fine addition to the Mexico City Zoo," she commented.

"The zoo can have it," Biff muttered.

Pendleton told everybody to go back to sleep and stop worrying. "It's almost unheard of for a snake of this size to invade an archaeological dig," he told them.

"This one," said Frank, "must have lost its way."

"Poor, crazy mixed-up snake," Joe said with a grin.

That broke up the tension and all the boys went back to their tents. In the morning, they joined Rose, Pendleton, and Courtney on a trek into the jungle in search of an armadillo. Pendleton wore the rough clothes and floppy hat of an experienced jungle guide. Courtney appeared in spotless white ducks, wearing his pith helmet and carrying his swagger stick.

"Melville, you'd better leave your helmet behind," Pendleton urged.

"It's part of one's dress in hot climates," was the reply. "I wish to dress correctly."

"That's when you're out in the sun. We'll be

under the trees and you'll need air. You'll be too hot with a helmet on."

Courtney insisted on wearing his helmet, however, so the guide shrugged and dropped the subject.

The party started their trek into the steaming jungle. Frank and Joe decided to say nothing but to keep their eyes open for a plane flying overhead. They might spot the one they suspected!

Soon they found themselves under a dense canopy of greenery. Branches, vines, moss, and creepers blotted out the sun. Much of the time the trekkers had to hack their way through with machetes. Birds and monkeys screamed at them from the trees, and weasels and other small creatures fled through the underbrush at their approach.

Insects stung them and sweat poured down their faces. As Pendleton had predicted, Courtney felt the heat worst of all because of his helmet.

"Ditch it!" the guide advised.

"A Hawkins man never gives up," Courtney replied.

"Have it your way, but we have quite a distance to go before we reach armadillo country."

They slogged forward, taking regular breaks since it was so difficult to advance. Late in the afternoon, the guide suggested, "Let's call it a day." The others willingly agreed. They opened crackers and tinned meat, and ate dinner.

Then Rose gave a talk on armadillos. "They're rarely found together," she stated. "When we spot an armadillo, we'll run him to earth. He'll try to reach the security of his burrow before you get there. If you head him off, he'll roll up into a ball and stay put."

"Why does he do that?" Tony queried.

Rose smiled. "He hopes that whoever is bothering him will get tired of waiting for him to uncurl and go away."

"What are the chances of finding one tomorrow?" Chet asked.

"Pretty good. Yucatán has been the home of the armadillo for thousands of years. According to a Mayan myth vultures turn into armadillos when they grow old. There are plenty left here."

In the morning, the march resumed. Insects swarmed around the hunters and Frank swatted a mosquito. "They're as big as robins," he complained.

"Big as crows," Joe corrected him, knocking one off his cheek.

After hours of pushing through the jungle, Rose noticed an anthill that had been broken open. "An armadillo did that," she said, excited. "Ants are number one on his menu."

Pendleton told the group to split up. "Look under bushes and in burrows. If you flush an armadillo, sing out. The rest of us will come on the run."

Courtney slapped his swagger stick against a tree. "I will direct the capture," he offered.

"I'll bet he will," Frank whispered to Joe. "He's not about to touch an armadillo."

They separated to look for their quarry. Rose tried to pick up a trail at the ravaged anthill. Pendleton continued straight ahead in the direction they had been taking. Courtney stabbed into the bushes with his swagger stick, looking as if he hoped never to see an armadillo in his life.

Chet, Biff, and Tony moved beyond Courtney into the jungle. Frank and Joe went to the left. "There's one thing we won't find in here," Frank remarked.

"What's that?"

"The Mexico City plane. You couldn't fit even a helicopter into this jungle with a shoehorn."

"That's right. Well, let's concentrate on the armadillo."

They split up. Frank vanished among some moss-laden trees. Joe took a route over a carpet of jungle vegetation. The undergrowth slowed him considerably. Vines caught his clothing, and creepers tripped him. A green parrot fluttered down onto a bush and squawked at him angrily, but he laughed as a hare stood upright on its hind legs, twitching its nose as he passed.

Presently Joe found an armadillo burrow, which he probed with a branch. It was empty. He went on, but after a while his legs were tired. He paused beside a tree in an open space of the jungle to rest. *Wham!* A rock slammed into the tree, inches from his head! It bounced off and caromed into a thicket.

Joe hit the ground in a headlong dive. He crawled over a tangle of creepers and pulled himself into a crouching position behind another tree. Gingerly he peered around the trunk. No one was in sight.

A sharp report cut through the stillness of the jungle. A shot! It had come from behind him! Joe dodged into the underbrush and stealthily moved in an arc toward the spot where the shot had been fired. He saw no one.

His companions had heard the shot, and ran up to see what had happened.

"Somebody used me for a clay pigeon," Joe told them. "He fired right at me!"

Frank turned to Pendleton. "You're the only one carrying a weapon. Did you fire at Joe?"

"Of course not." The jungle guide strenuously denied the charge. He opened the breech of his rifle. "Look for yourself. It hasn't been fired."

"Who could it be, then?" Biff wondered.

Tony sighed. "We're obviously not the only ones here in the wilderness."

"Maybe it was a Mayan hunter after armadillo," Pendleton suggested. "Mayas love armadillo steaks."

"Or the guy who dug the hole and tried to conk

us with a tree," Frank said to Joe in a low voice. "Matter of fact, that's more likely."

"That would mean we're being watched constantly," Joe said in alarm.

Frank nodded. "It is a possibility."

The searchers began beating the undergrowth. An armadillo, evidently startled, bolted from behind a rock. It was about three feet long, with a pointed snout, long ears, and a long tail. The armor fitted over its back like a half shell.

The animal hit Biff a hard blow on the ankles, knocking him off his feet, then raced past. Everybody chased the armadillo, careening and stumbling through the jungle undergrowth.

The creature veered into Chet's path. As he lunged for it, his foot caught in a creeper, and he fell with a crash. The Hardys, too close behind him to stop, piled on top of the stout boy in a tangle of arms and legs. Frantically they scrambled to their feet and resumed the chase.

The armadillo did an about-face and raced between them. It plowed into Courtney, bowling the Hawkins man over. His pith helmet rolled into the underbrush. He got to his feet slowly, retrieved the helmet, brushed it with his sleeve, and placed it on his head, looking embarrassed.

"I shan't associate with any armadillo," he declared, seating himself on a stump and rapping it with his swagger stick. "I will wait here."

The animal reached its burrow, but Pendleton,

too quick for it, seized the armadillo and pulled it out, kicking and squealing. The creature resisted briefly before quieting down in the guide's arms.

The other searchers arrived. The boys stroked the armor, which was composed of hide with a series of plates around the body, giving it flexibility.

"So that's an armadillo!" Tony marveled.

"Yes indeed," Rose answered. She scratched its ears with her fingertips.

"Isn't that dangerous?" Chet asked apprehensively. "You might lose a finger."

Rose shook her head. "Armadillos have few or no front teeth, so they can't bite." She held the animal while Pendleton took a collapsible wire cage from his pack. They eased their captive into it and the jungle guide pulled the straps over his shoulders. The cage rode easily on his back.

"Mission accomplished," Pendleton said.

"Right-o!" Courtney exclaimed. "We may now leave this jungle, of which I have had quite enough."

Frank spoke. "I'd like to scout around here a bit longer."

Joe and his friends agreed enthusiastically, but Pendleton objected. "We'll have to get back to the dig. Do you want to stay here alone?"

"Is there any reason why we shouldn't?"

"Not really. We're on an elevation where the

mosquitoes aren't bad. I don't think you'll see any dangerous animals, either. Can you find your way back to camp?"

"Sure," Frank said. "We'll go by the compass. Since we came from a northeasterly direction, we'll return that way."

"Good enough," Pendleton replied. "You stay then, and we'll be on our way."

Courtney doffed his pith helmet. *"Adios,"* he said solemnly, and Rose waved good-by.

As the three explorers disappeared into the jungle, their footsteps died away in the distance.

The boys walked in the opposite direction, noting the jungle flowers and animals as they went.

"There are a million monkeys here," Biff judged.

"And a billion parrots," Tony added.

"What do we do if we meet any Mayas?" Joe asked.

"Talk Mayan to them," Frank quipped.

By nightfall the boys were extremely tired. Making a hasty meal of their rations, they set up camp beneath towering trees.

Frank could not sleep. He kept thinking about the strange events that had taken Joe and him to Switzerland, then to the jungles of Yucatán. It appeared that they were finally onto a clue—the plane marked "Mexico City." But where was it?

He sat up and turned his head. Everything was

pitch black. Suddenly through the darkness he saw a light. It moved in a circle and went out. Frank rubbed his eyes.

The light flashed once more, swaying back and forth for a few minutes, then went out again. In a moment the signal was repeated a third time.

Now fully awake, Frank reached over and shook his brother.

Joe yawned. "What is it, Frank?"

"A light out there! Look!"

The beam remained stationary for a few seconds. Then it started moving once more, vanished, and reappeared a moment later.

Frank jumped up. "Hurry, Joe, we'll have to find out what this means!" He grabbed his compass and the two slipped through the jungle, guiding themselves by the mysterious light. After about half a mile, they reached a clearing.

The full moon revealed a weird sight. A stone building covered with jungle vegetation towered toward the sky. The vines and creepers spreading up the uncanny edifice from base to summit seemed like writhing serpents and disguised the building completely. The mysterious beam came from the summit.

"That's a flashlight!" Joe said in a low voice. "Somebody's up there. What's he doing, Frank?"

"Joe, I believe he's signaling a pal. But why?"

CHAPTER XII

The Jungle Pyramid

THE Hardys entered the clearing and cautiously approached the eerie edifice. It was more than a hundred feet high, tapered toward the summit, with indented rows of stone steps rising from the bottom to the top. The base was formed of massive stone blocks. On the summit stood a temple.

"I'll bet it's the lost pyramid!" Frank gaped.

"No wonder it got lost," Joe whispered. "Rose was right. The jungle covers everything!"

Close up, they could see where winds had blown earth over the stone blocks. The seeds of plants, vines, creepers, shrubs, and flowers had imbedded themselves in the earth and sprouted in profusion.

Joe looked up toward the light on the summit. "Let's find out what's going on," he whispered.

"Easy does it," Frank counseled. "We don't want to scare the person off. First we'll explore the ground around the pyramid. Whoever is up there might be signaling an accomplice down here."

Stealthily the two boys slunk past the staircase in the center of the façade, noting that it lead up to the temple entrance. As they turned the corner, Joe bumped into an upright slab of stone covered with raised squares and bearing strange symbols.

"Glyphs," he thought.

They went on with their search. At the back of the pyramid, they saw the carved figure of a monstrous snake undulating down over the stone blocks. Eyes of obsidian glinted at them in the semidarkness. The open mouth revealed oversized fangs. Plumes bedecked the head and neck.

"The Feathered Serpent of the Mayas!" Frank said.

He and Joe had seen statues of this mythical creature many times since their arrival in Mexico. They knew it was the principal god of the Indians who had lived in Mexico before Columbus came to America.

Circling the pyramid, the boys returned to their starting point. "Nobody down here but us," Joe said in a low voice.

The light was still showing on the summit. Suddenly, at the door of the temple, it went out.

"The man's gone inside," Frank observed. "This is our chance."

Slipping and sliding, the Hardys silently climbed the steps to the top of the pyramid. Frank edged his way into the entrance of the temple. They did not see the light, and he whispered, "Maybe there are inner stairs to the top."

"Then we can take him by surprise," Joe said. He stepped forward, feeling his way along the wall. The boys did not want to use their pencil flashlights because they might alert the person inside to the fact that they were stalking him.

Suddenly Joe plummeted out of sight!

"Joe!" Frank whispered hoarsely. "Joe! Where are you? Joe!"

Receiving no answer, Frank fished out his light and played the beam across the interior. At his feet the edge of a long stone incline dropped into utter darkness. Frank was horrified. Had Joe plunged down into a Mayan dungeon? If so, he might be hurt! He might be unconscious! He might even be—! "Joe!" he called. "Are you all right?"

Then he heard Joe's voice behind him. "I'm okay, Frank. I just took a ride on a Mayan roller coaster!"

Frank breathed easier.

"It's leading outside to the steps in the back," Joe continued. "I landed next to the Feathered Serpent. He didn't blink an eye."

Frank kept the beam of his flashlight shining over the end of the inclined plane. The boys decided it must have been used to lever heavy objects up to the higher levels of the pyramid.

"No freight elevators for the Mayas," Joe joked. "They did everything with muscle."

"Not so loud!" Frank warned. He played his beam around the lower chamber of the temple. It flashed over a pile of clay pots and stone figures in a corner.

"Where are we?" Joe asked.

"It looks like a storeroom, Joe. They kept supplies here until they were needed upstairs." The flashlight crossed a tall stone column in the opposite corner. Frank brought it back into focus. The column was a rectangular stone block standing on end, about as tall as the boys. The same face was repeated four times from top to bottom, the visage of a large cat, its fangs bared in a savage snarl. "The jaguar god," Frank whispered.

"As Chet would say, I hope I never meet up with him," Joe said.

Frank now pointed his flashlight toward the ceiling. It showed row after row of petroglyphs, which they could not read.

"I understand," Frank said, "that Mayan script has not been completely deciphered yet."

The Hardys circled the chamber. The only opening was a low doorway. Frank ducked under it, followed by Joe, into a small, empty room. A quick search showed it had no other outlet.

A rustle at the doorway made Frank snap off his flashlight. The boys whirled in the defensive stance of karate experts. The sound came directly toward them in the darkness!

The Hardys had a strategy for such confrontations. They counted silently to three, then Frank snapped on his light. At the same time, Joe leaped on the intruder. He received a whiplash across the face, and went down in a tangle of branches!

Frank chuckled in spite of the danger. "A bush! The wind blew it in here!"

Ruefully Joe extricated himself and got to his feet. "Next time, I'll look before I leap!" he said.

The Hardys went back through the first chamber. "We'll have to use the outer stairs to get to the top of the temple," Frank declared. "I hope the guy inside won't see or hear us."

He pocketed his flashlight; then the boys went outside and maneuvered over to the staircase. The steps seemed to rise endlessly above them, steep and narrow. The footing was difficult, and clouds gathering across the face of the moon created a dark, murky atmosphere.

"Don't fall!" Frank muttered. "It's a bumpy road to the ground."

They got about a third of the way up, gripping vines to steady themselves and making sure of a foothold on every step, before they were interrupted. Something moved among the vines near Frank's right hand. Pulling his fingers away, he got out his light and shone the beam on the fluttering leaves. A menacing snake raised its head, stared at him for a few seconds, then slithered onto the bough of a small tree. It vanished among the creepers.

Frank felt his heart pounding. He had almost placed his hand on a fer-de-lance, one of the most poisonous snakes of the Yucatán jungle!

"You're no snake charmer," Joe whispered.

"Don't fool around with our lethal companions."

They resumed their climb. A black object hurtled through the air at them. Joe ducked in time to avoid getting hit on the head, but lost his footing and toppled off the step! Frank grabbed his brother in midair and held him until he could regain his foothold.

The trajectile veered to one side and landed on a bush. A harsh croak jarred their ears.

"A raven!" Frank whispered. "He almost got us!" As they continued their climb close to the summit, Frank paused and looked up. The smoother stone of the temple gleamed through tangled tropical growth that sprouted on its roof and spilled down the sides, waving wildly in a rising wind. The entrance was a dark oblong in the front wall. Total silence reigned over the jungle pyramid.

Frank gestured to Joe not to make a sound. They moved slowly and carefully up the rest of the steps. The final one brought them to the sacrificial chamber. On it stood a platform with four feet on each side. The walls of the temple behind it were made of pink-red stone rising some twenty feet into the air. A doorway led into the interior, and blank walls extended on each side of the doorway. The roof was flat.

Frank and Joe stole to one side of the entrance and peered in cautiously. A shaft of moonlight gleamed through an opening in the opposite wall.

There was no sign or sound of life in the temple.

"Do you think the guy heard us and ran?" Joe asked in a whisper.

"Well, if he did, let's see what he was up to," Frank said.

As the boys entered, Frank fumbled for his flashlight. Just then something rustled in a dark corner, and the next instant a man barreled out at them! He leveled Joe with a wild swing, then grappled with Frank!

The pair staggered back and forth in a furious test of strength until the assailant gave ground. Frank pressed him back. They swayed through the doorway and over to the staircase.

Joe recovered slowly from the blow. He felt woozy, but got to his feet. Then he realized he was alone in the temple. His brother and their attacker were gone!

"Frank!" he shouted. "Frank!"

The name echoed out over the jungle, but Frank did not answer. Frantically Joe rushed through the nearest doorway, which was the rear exit, and circled around the temple to the front.

There he could see Frank and the stranger still locked in combat! Joe rushed to help his brother, but before he could reach the spot, Frank and his attacker had lost their footing!

With a scream, they pitched down the main staircase and fell toward the bottom of the jungle pyramid!

CHAPTER XIII

A Strange Figure

JOE leaped forward and clutched wildly at Frank, but his fingers missed by inches!

Three new shapes were suddenly visible on the steps in the moonlight. Three pairs of arms caught Frank and his antagonist in midair. With great relief, Joe recognized Chet, Biff, and Tony!

The boys pulled Frank free. He stood to one side, panting from his struggle, while Biff gripped his adversary in a bear hug. The two wrestled fiercely on the temple staircase.

The man tripped Biff, who tumbled into a tangle of creepers. The assailant leaped up the steps, but Tony brought him down with a tackle around the ankles. Chet sat on him and grinned.

"Had enough?" Chet inquired.

"Chet's a bit overweight," Tony pointed out.

"I—can—tell—that!" the man gasped. "Okay. I give up!"

The boys pushed their captive up to the summit and backed him against the temple wall in the darkness.

"You guys came just in time," Frank said to his friends. "How did you get here?"

Biff said he had awakened to discover that Frank and Joe were gone. "I noticed a light and figured you must have seen it, too. So I woke Chet and Tony and we decided to back you up in case you were in trouble. We found what we think is the lost pyramid, and we saw a hassle on the top."

"We came up the Mayan escalator," Tony quipped. "Stone blocks and leg power."

Biff looked at their captive. "Say, who is this guy?"

Joe took out his pencil flashlight, snapped it on, and shone it in the man's face.

Rumble Murphy!

"What are you doing here?" Frank asked the pilot.

"None of your business!" Murphy grunted.

"Let's tie him up," Frank suggested. "One of us can watch him, while the rest are searching the place. There should be some clue as to what our friend was doing in the pyramid."

The boys handcuffed Murphy with Joe's belt, and tied his ankles with Tony's. Biff volunteered to guard the pilot, while the others would go over the temple and pyramid with a fine-toothed comb, using their flashlights.

First they entered the section of the temple where they had been before. It had a high ceiling.

A raised altar stood at one end and a row of stone idols at the other. Here the priests of the Mayan religion apparently had presided over ceremonies to the gods.

"Wow!" Tony said as he played his light over the altar. "This is where the Indians prayed to the jaguar god and the feathered serpent."

Frank nodded. "Right now I'm not interested in the feathered serpent, but in some clues to why Murphy was here."

The boys looked in every nook and cranny, and were about to give up when Joe called out, "Hey, fellows! Come over here!"

The others ran up to him. Joe pointed to a bulky sack concealed behind a statue of the jaguar god. Together, the boys dragged it into the center of the room.

"It's heavy as lead!" Tony exclaimed.

Excited, they opened it.

"Gold!" Chet cried in awe as they pulled out one object after another. First came a disc representing the sun. Small figurines followed. Finally there were dozens of ornaments—headdresses, bracelets, and rings.

"I don't believe it!" Frank said. "This stuff is priceless!"

"All Mayan," Chet added. "It takes an adept in golden artifacts to know that."

Joe upended the sack and shook out the contents. "The Scythian horse isn't here," he said, a note of disappointment in his voice.

"This stuff is priceless!" Frank said.

But Chet was ecstatic. "Who cares! You were looking for one little figurine, and see what you've found instead!"

"Not the Wakefield gold, either," Frank said.

"Let's take one thing at a time," Tony suggested, "and confront Rumble Murphy with the evidence. Maybe he'll enlighten us as to the origin of this treasure."

"Good idea," Frank said, and the boys began putting the glittering objects back into the sack.

"Remember the fortune-teller in Mexico City?" Joe asked his brother. "She said there was much gold in your future. Maybe she meant this."

Frank laughed. "Who knows?"

The boys carried the sack outside and showed it to Biff. Murphy mumbled under his breath.

"Okay, Murphy," Frank said. "You may as well tell us what this is all about."

Murphy glared as his captors surrounded him menacingly.

"Come on, talk!" Biff hissed and moved his bulky figure closer to the pilot.

"All right, all right," Murphy grumbled. "I handle Mayan artifacts. Jeep them to Chichén Itzá, then fly them out of Mexico for international buyers."

"Did you ever see a figurine of a rearing horse?" Tony inquired. "A Scythian piece."

Murphy shook his head. "I told you I handle only stuff that's found right here in Mexico— Aztec, Mayan, Olmec—no Scythian gold."

"How did you find the pyramid?" Frank queried.

"I spotted it one day when I was flying low over the jungle. Later I discovered a way in by jeep from Chichén Itzá. And I saw it was the perfect hideout because nobody else knew where it was, so I stored my loot here."

Frank changed the line of questioning. "Why did you threaten us at the airport in Mexico City?"

"Because your fat friend said you were after my gold!"

"*Your* gold?" Frank was puzzled.

"He said you always find your man, and you'd find the gold. I don't know anyone else smuggling gold around here, so I figured you were after me! Who do you work for, anyway?"

Frank grinned. "The Wakefield Mint."

"What!"

"Never mind. But we had nothing to do with you. If you hadn't signaled tonight, we would never have suspected you."

Murphy mumbled again, but said nothing aloud.

Biff said, "You were the one who dug the hole in the trail from Chichén Itzá and then caused the tree to tumble on us! You almost killed us!"

"I did no such thing," Murphy grumbled, but the boys knew he was lying.

"And you tampered with the engine of our chartered plane," Joe accused. "After you dug the hole you flew back to Mexico City and waited for us!"

"And you took a pot shot at Joe today," Frank added.

Murphy did not reply.

"Why were you signaling with the flashlight tonight?" Frank asked.

"What signal?" Murphy asked defiantly.

"Don't play dumb," Frank said. "If we hadn't seen your light, we never would have found you or the pyramid."

"A buddy of mine flies over here at night at a certain time to let me know if we found a buyer. I don't know which night he's coming, so I signal, then he drops the instructions. He didn't show up tonight."

"Why did you take a chance with us so close by?" Tony asked.

"I didn't know you were still here," Murphy said glumly. "I thought you had left with the others."

By now the sun had begun to rise and a soft mist hung over the jungle.

"What'll we do with him?" Chet asked.

"Murphy must have a jeep around," Frank replied. "We'll have to deliver him to the nearest police station in Chichén Itzá."

Rumble Murphy looked at them with squinting eyes. "Do you have to be that drastic? Look, I could cut you in on the loot. This stuff is worth a bundle of money. If you don't want to handle it

yourselves, I'll pay you in cash. Fifty-fifty. What
do you say?"

"No," Frank said laconically.

"All right. I'll give you seventy-five percent.
That's robbing me, but what can I do?"

"Forget it, Murphy," Joe said. "We're not
thieves."

"You're crazy! Do you realize what you're turning down? Listen, I'll give you everything, but
don't take me to the cops!"

Frank ignored the plea. "Where's your jeep?"

Murphy realized that he had lost and started to
scream at the top of his lungs. Suddenly he fell
silent and would not utter another word.

"I'll go find the jeep," Frank offered. "It has to
be around here somewhere. Hey, look!"

He pointed to a stranger entering the trampled
area around the pyramid. He was a man dressed
in the white suit worn by modern Mayas, with a
wide-brimmed straw hat on his head. He edged
around the pyramid in a suspicious manner.

"So, there's your accomplice, Murphy!" Joe
exclaimed. "Let's meet him, gang. Biff, want to
guard our friend again?"

"Sure thing," Biff replied as Frank, Joe, and
Chet took the steps down as fast as they could,
followed by Tony. They circled the pyramid,
taking the direction opposite that used by the man
in the white suit.

They met him at the corner. He had the light-
copper coloring of an Indian. Lank black hair ex-

tended down to his shoulders. His cheeks were round and a scar ran across the right side of his face. He looked startled when he saw them.

"Are you looking for Rumble Murphy?" Joe asked.

The man responded in a rapid flow of Spanish. Though the boys had studied the language in high school, they could not follow him because he spoke so fast and with a strange inflection. Joe asked him to repeat slowly what he had just said, but the man stared at him blankly.

Chet had an idea. "Let's try sign language," he suggested. "I'll take it from here."

He touched the man on the shoulder, turned, and pointed into the jungle. He made a long sweep with one arm toward the pyramid.

"What does that mean?" Joe wondered.

"I'm asking him where he comes from, and how he got here," Chet explained.

"Well, you could have fooled me," Joe said.

The man smiled, shrugged, and spoke again.

"We're getting nowhere fast," Frank protested.

The boys decided to bring the man face to face with Murphy. One of them might give something away. They were discussing the best way to arrange the confrontation when the man suddenly spoke English.

"Bayport seems to be on the ball!"

CHAPTER XIV

The Aztec War God

THE boys gaped. The voice was unmistakably that of their father!

"Dad!" Frank cried out. "I don't believe it!" He scrutinized the coppery face closely. Then he grinned. "I should have known. The color of your eyes doesn't fit your make-up!"

Mr. Hardy chuckled. "A bit of make-up and cheek pads can do a lot to change one's appearance. And I can always squint when necessary."

"But, Dad, we thought you were investigating the case in Wakefield," Joe said. "What's up?"

"It's a long story," Mr. Hardy said. "And it was John Armstrong's idea."

"You mean he doesn't trust us?" Frank asked.

"Well, he thought you could use some reinforcement. Actually, he decided all of a sudden that I was wasting my time in Wakefield. Since he had some business in Mexico City, he asked me to come along. We left the day after you did. When we arrived, John took care of his appointment in the city, while I asked questions around the airport about the mysterious plane."

"Same as we did," Joe said. "And that's how you found out about Palango?"

"Palango? What's that?"

"An archaeological dig near here," Frank said. "That's where we ended up."

Mr. Hardy shook his head. "No one mentioned Palango to me. But I was tipped off that Rumble Murphy was smuggling gold, so I hid in his plane all the way to Mérida."

"Wow!" Chet looked at the detective in admiration. "Neat sleuthing!"

"Well, I almost lost him when we arrived," Mr. Hardy continued. "I had to rent a jeep while his was already waiting. But I caught up with him and followed him here."

"Did he stop on the way?" Frank asked.

"Yes, in the jungle, for about an hour. He got out of his jeep and disappeared into the woods. Then another car came along the trail, nearly ran into a hole, and barely escaped a falling tree. I saw it from a distance."

"That car was ours!" Frank cried out.

Mr. Hardy stared at the boys. "You'd better tell me all that's happened to you," he said gravely.

The boys described their adventures for their father, then Joe asked, "Dad, what did you do when you saw the pyramid?"

"There wasn't much I could do," Mr. Hardy said. "I pitched a tent nearby and kept observing Murphy so I could be sure he didn't have a gang of people working here with him. Yesterday he left the place and I followed him into the jungle. There were people close by and he shot at something, maybe to scare them off."

"He shot at me!" Joe declared. "But he didn't scare us away!"

Mr. Hardy nodded. "I was hoping he'd leave for a while so I could search the pyramid, but he went right back."

"Did you see the lights last night?" Frank asked.

"No. I must have dozed off. This morning I decided I'd better do something. So I disguised myself and was on the way to confront Murphy when I met you."

"We've taken care of Murphy already, Mr. Hardy," Chet announced and they reported their adventure of the previous night.

"Murphy admits he's a smuggler," Biff said. "We found his loot. Great stuff—gold by the sackful!"

"Unfortunately it wasn't the Wakefield gold, or the Scythian figurine, either," Frank said.

Mr. Hardy tried to cheer his son. "Even if Murphy and Palango were false leads, you discovered an illegal smuggling operation. The Mexican government will be very grateful to you, and Murphy deserves to be put out of business."

Frank nodded. "You're right. We were just

about to take him to Chichén Itzá and hand him over to the police. If necessary, we'll take him to Mérida."

"Good thinking. We can use his jeep and mine. Let's go get him," Mr. Hardy said.

The group walked up the steps of the pyramid to where Biff was guarding Murphy. Biff marveled at Mr. Hardy's disguise, and the thief glowered at them. "I want to see a lawyer," he snarled.

"You'll see one in town, Murphy," Mr. Hardy said. "First we'll take you and your loot out of here."

The boys untied Murphy's ankles and led him to their father's jeep. He was put in the front seat, while Tony and Biff rode in the back to make sure the smuggler would not try to escape.

The others had soon located Murphy's vehicle and Frank climbed behind the wheel with Joe and Chet as passengers. The jeeps took a long detour that Murphy had discovered was the easiest route through the jungle. Arriving in Chichén Itzá, they turned the man and his gold over to the authorities.

The police deputy was gratified. "We knew a smuggler was operating in this area, but we never could catch him. You have done us a great favor!"

After Murphy was led away, Frank said. "I don't see any reason to go back to Palango. What do you think, Dad?"

"I agree. Let's drive to Mérida and get a flight from there to Mexico City. Then we can see what Armstrong has in mind."

In Mérida, Mr. Hardy called John Armstrong at his hotel to tell him when they would arrive. He picked them up at the airport. Looking harried, he mopped his brow with his handkerchief.

"What's new, Fenton?" he asked.

"No news of the mint thief, John. We didn't find the stolen gold in the jungle," Mr. Hardy replied, "but the boys nabbed a smuggler." He told Armstrong about their adventure.

Armstrong sighed. "While you were away, I checked with the police on Zemog. Nothing positive there either. But I'm sure the answer—"

"Look!" Joe interrupted and pointed to a small plane with the words "Mexico City" on the fuselage. It was just taking off on the runway.

Joe memorized the craft's number, and the excited boys went to check with the control tower. They found out that the plane belonged to Carlos Calderón. According to the pilot's flight plan, he was bound for Mérida.

"I think he's going to Palango," the official in the tower told them.

"Results at last!" Joe said jubilantly as they went back to tell their father and Armstrong what they had just heard.

Armstrong was enthusiastic. "You see? We'll have to go there right away!"

They took a flight the following morning. Mr. Hardy would stay in Mexico City to testify against Murphy, who was being transferred for his hearing the next day. Armstrong and the boys flew to Mérida, where they rented two jeeps and once more drove to the dig. When they arrived, their archaeological friends greeted them with loud shouts.

"Thank goodness you're all right!" Rose cried out. "We thought you were lost in the jungle! Frank Pendleton went out looking for you but had no luck!"

"We ran into an unexpected adventure," Frank said. After introducing John Armstrong, he told about Rumble Murphy and the pyramid.

Steve Weiss was incredulous. "This is absolutely fantastic!" he said.

"Well, we didn't find what we were after," Frank said. "But the plane we were looking for has supposedly flown to Mérida and its owner, Carlos Calderón, was planning to come here."

"Carlos!" Steve exclaimed. "He's a good friend of ours, an archaeology student who visits once in a while. He does graduate work at the University of Mexico. Right now he's out in the jungle with a couple of our men. Should be back any minute, however."

"Why didn't you tell us his plane had 'Mexico City' on it?" Joe asked.

"I didn't know. He told us he bought a small plane recently, but I never saw it."

Just then three men appeared at the excavation site. Two were Mexican workmen, the third a handsome young fellow with wavy black hair and a bright smile.

"Hey, Carlos!" Steve called out. "These people want to meet you."

He introduced everyone, then Frank asked Carlos if he had ever been in Wakefield, U.S.A.

The young man was surprised. "No, I have never been out of Mexico. Why do you ask?"

"We're trailing a private plane marked 'Mexico City' that took off from an airstrip near Wakefield."

"When was that?" Carlos asked.

Frank gave him the date.

"Wait a minute," Weiss intervened. "At that time Carlos was here at the Palango dig with us."

Melville Courtney had been listening. Now he slapped his swagger stick against his boot and addressed the boys. "My dear chaps, you will have to look elsewhere for your culprit. My goodness, how suspicious you are!"

"I realize you have a case to solve," Steve Weiss said. "But I hope you'll stay and lead us to the lost pyramid. We'll go out tomorrow and do a preliminary survey. After that we'll take a work gang and begin clearing away the vegetation."

Frank and Joe looked at Armstrong, who nodded vigorously. "Of course we'll stay. We'll be glad to guide you to the place." To Frank he said in a low tone, "I don't believe Calderón is as harmless as he seems. Maybe someone else flew his plane. We'll stay here and keep him under surveillance."

Steve Weiss and his group were excited about the lost pyramid, and they could hardly wait to explore it. "We're glad you caught that smuggler," Steve told the boys. "We just dug up a lot of artifacts, and he might have stolen them. Look here." He showed them small statues, images of the Mayan gods, an assortment of weapons and knives, and some tablets bearing petroglyphic inscriptions.

"This is our masterpiece," he declared, holding one up for all to see. "It's an image of the Aztec war god. The Aztecs traded with the Mayas of Yucatán, you know."

The image was a shining gold mask. The features were contorted into a ferocious scowl, and the jade eyes reflected the sunlight in shimmering blue-green.

Weiss handed the mask to Frank, who examined it and passed the piece around the circle. Everybody was thrilled by the Aztec war god. Chet and Carlos were fascinated.

Armstrong hefted the mask. "Feels like solid gold," he announced. "I'd say it's as valuable as one of our larger bars in the mint."

He began to speak with Chet, Carlos, and Pendleton about the quality of gold. Later that evening, the four sat up after the others had gone to bed. Just before he fell asleep, Joe heard Chet retire to his tent.

A rattling noise woke Joe up hours later. It came from the tent where the artifacts were kept. Somebody was banging them together as if searching for something! Silently Joe crept toward the tent, straining his eyes to see in the darkness. A figure stole out and walked toward the jungle.

Dark clouds floated past overhead. Moonlight gleamed on a gold mask molded into a ferocious scowl.

"Whoever he is," Joe thought, "he's stealing the valuable gold mask!"

CHAPTER XV

Lethal Reptiles

FOR a moment Joe stared at the thief, who was slowly strolling along in the darkness. Then the young detective crept back to his tent and awakened Frank.

"Someone's taking off with the golden mask!" he whispered into his brother's ear. "We'd better stop him!"

Frank bolted out of his sleeping bag. "Go after him," he said. "I'll wake the others and we'll be right there."

Joe ran from the camp as quietly as he could in order not to alert the thief. The man might run into the jungle and disappear into the night! He saw the thief, still walking slowly in the moonlight, and caught up to him. "Stop!" Joe commanded. "Don't go any farther!"

He expected the thief to whirl around and attack him, and was ready to fight. Instead, the man turned slowly, holding the mask over his face, and said nothing!

By now Frank and the others ran up. "Joe, did you get him?" Frank called out.

"Right here," Joe replied.

"Who is he?" Steve Weiss demanded.

Joe stared at the thief, who stood motionless, his face hidden behind the ancient image. "Come on," Joe said, "take that thing away and stop playing games!"

The man did not move. Joe grabbed the mask and pulled it from the thief's face.

Carlos Calderón!

"Carlos, what are you doing with that mask?" Steve Weiss asked, incredulous. "You're not trying to steal it, are you?"

"Of course he is," Armstrong declared. "He took it and then tried to make a getaway. I suspected him all along!"

Weiss took the mask from Joe. "I don't know the explanation," he said, "but Carlos is not a thief. I'm sure of that."

"Weiss, you're out of your mind," Armstrong exploded. "We've caught him red-handed!"

Carlos stood perfectly still, saying nothing. He looked at the rest with a fixed stare.

"He's sleepwalking!" Tony exclaimed.

"No, that's not it," Frank said. "A sleepwalker would have awakened after all this commotion."

Rose walked up to Carlos. She peered deep into

his eyes, made passes with her hand in front of his face, and spoke to him. He did not react.

"He's in a trance," the biologist said. "I think Carlos has been hypnotized. I've studied the subject and I know all the signs. A hypnotized person looks just the way Carlos does."

Frank became excited. "Somebody hypnotized Carlos and made him take the gold mask!"

Chet scratched his head. "But who?"

"Nobody in this camp," Weiss said. "None of us is a hypnotist."

"Could it be somebody hiding in the jungle?" Tony suggested. "The guy met Carlos, hypnotized him, and told him to get the mask. A confederate of Rumble Murphy's, perhaps."

"You may be right," Joe said. "It's one more mystery for us to solve."

Weiss tapped a finger against his chin. "I've just thought of something. Aztec masks of the gods were supposed to have a hypnotic effect on worshippers in the temples. I wonder if the mask could have hypnotized Carlos."

"Nonsense!" Armstrong objected. "He wasn't in a trance when I left him last night. He stole the mask deliberately!"

"Why not ask him?" Biff suggested. He shook the student. "Carlos! Wake up!" he commanded. "Wake up!"

Carlos did not respond.

"It's no use," Rose said. "He can't hear you. Besides, it's dangerous to wake up a hypnotized person suddenly. It could affect his mind and impair his memory. Let him sleep it off."

"Just like that?" Pendleton queried.

"Right. Most hypnotized people pass into ordinary sleep and wake up normally. In extreme cases, a doctor is needed. All we can do is see how Carlos comes out of this."

Weiss led the way back to camp. Rose guided Carlos by the elbow. She deposited him in his tent while Steve replaced the gold mask with the rest of the artifacts from the dig.

"I'll stand guard outside Calderón's tent," John Armstrong offered, "and make sure he doesn't escape."

The others went back to sleep. In the morning, Carlos came out of his tent to join the group for breakfast. Armstrong, who was still on guard, grabbed him.

"Hey, let go of me!" the student objected. "What's the idea? I can walk on my own."

"We saw that last night," Armstrong replied sarcastically.

"What are you talking about?"

"About the way you tried to walk off with the gold mask!"

"John, you don't make any sense at all," Carlos said, looking puzzled. "*You* took the mask back to the tent before we went to bed, not I!"

"Come on, the others will tell you," Armstrong said, dragging the student to the breakfast area.

Everyone seemed to stare at him in a strange

way. Carlos began to feel uncomfortable. "Is anything wrong?" he asked. "John said something about my walking off with the mask. What is this?"

"Carlos, what is the last thing you remember last night?" Frank Hardy asked.

"Well, Chet, John, Pendleton, and I talked about the mask and admired the beautiful craftsmanship. Then John took it back to the artifacts tent and we all went to bed."

"And then?"

"Then? Nothing. I went to sleep! What in the world are you getting at?"

"You walked off into the jungle with the mask in the middle of the night," Armstrong said. "Don't deny it because we all saw you!"

Carlos stared at the man in utter astonishment, then turned to Steve Weiss. "Steve," he said, and his voice was shaking with fear and bewilderment, "what is this man trying to do to me? You know I'm not a thief. I didn't touch that mask after I went to my tent. You people all know me. Please, won't anyone stick up for me?"

Rose walked over to the student and put her arm around his shoulders. "Calm down, Carlos. Something happened last night, and we have a pretty good idea what. You were hypnotized and started to walk away from the camp with the mask. Moreover you didn't react to anything we said to you."

"Hypnotized! But—but I don't remember anything of the sort."

"You wouldn't, so don't worry about it."

Carlos sat down and put his head into his hands. "I can't believe it. I just can't believe it."

Armstrong did not speak out loud, but said to Frank in a low voice, "I don't either. I think he's putting on an excellent show. Let's ask the authorities to investigate his story."

Frank was inclined to believe Carlos, but since he worked for Armstrong, he did not contradict him. "Sure, Mr. Armstrong, we'll check him out as soon as we get back to Mexico City."

Carlos stood up again and looked at everyone at the table. "Who hypnotized me?"

"We don't know," Steve said. "Must have been an outsider who stole in here."

"I haven't talked to any outsiders since I arrived!" Carlos argued.

"Who knows?" Pendleton put in. "Someone could have come into your tent last night and commanded you under hypnosis not to remember ever meeting him."

"But why would anyone want to do that?"

"Possibly so that you would take the mask and deposit it somewhere in the jungle."

"What—what if it happens again?"

"It won't. We'll keep an eye on you. Relax," Steve told him. "And now let's get to work. We're going to find the pyramid today. Remember?"

He organized a party, including Pendleton, the Hardys, and himself. Armstrong decided to watch Carlos; and Biff, Tony, and Chet would help Courtney to list artifacts from the dig.

"We don't have to hike as we did last time," Frank said. "I have a pretty good idea of how to find Murphy's trail from here. Let's take the jeep."

Frank found the way without difficulty, and even though it was a roundabout route from Palango, the searchers reached the pyramid within a few hours.

The archaeologist and the guide were ecstatic. "This is absolutely phenomenal!" Steve Weiss exclaimed. "We've finally found the lost pyramid! Frank, Joe, you can't imagine how grateful we are to you!"

The Hardys grinned. "Don't forget, we discovered it by accident!"

While Steve and Pendleton entered the structure, Frank and Joe reconnoitered the jungle around it and plunged into the underbrush.

"I believe Carlos was hypnotized," Frank said. "What do you think, Joe?"

"I'm with you. I hope whoever did it won't come back and put all of us in a trance!" He took out his machete and began to hack through the jungle growth. Frank did the same. The keen blades of the long knives easily sliced through the vegetation, lopping off vines, creepers, and tree branches.

The boys reached a clearing, where they paused for a conference on what to do next. "If we go any farther," Frank said, "we might lose our way. The undergrowth is dense around here. How about going back?"

Joe nodded. "Look! There's a path. Want to try it?"

"Sure. Why not?"

The new route took them downhill into a swampy region of the jungle. They found a sluggish creek and tramped along its banks until it widened into a fast-moving stream.

A steamy haze rose from the ground. Black mud clung to their shoes. Grassy hillocks were slick with wet grass, and tree boles slanted crazily from the bank out over the water. Moss hung from the branches like long, heavy ropes.

"Let's pretend we're monkeys," Joe proposed. "We'll swing from one tree to another on the moss and avoid getting our feet wet."

Frank chuckled. "Okay, Tarzan, you lead the way. I'll follow when I see how you make out."

Frank tripped over a root, and fell headlong into the ooze, breaking his fall with his hands. He pushed himself up into a squatting position and washed himself in the stream before proceeding.

The boys hiked along the stream, which flowed roughly in the direction of the pyramid. Massive tree roots compelled them to make a detour inland. They came to a rocky ledge, where ferns covered the mouth of a small cave.

Joe poked a branch into the darkness of the cave. *Whoosh!* A black snarling form flashed out at him! He ducked by reflex action. The creature just missed his head and zoomed up onto a branch overhead. Savage eyes glared down at him. Sharp fangs snapped.

"It's a bat!" Frank exclaimed.

Joe shuddered. "A vampire bat. Let's get out of here before his buddies in the cave come out!"

They hurried around to the bank and continued tramping downstream. The river gradually broadened until it extended a hundred yards across. The Hardys stopped to survey it.

A snout broke the surface and rose into the air, revealing a long head with tiny reptilian eyes. The body floated like a log. A pair of jaws opened, revealing a row of wicked fangs. A heavy tail whiplashed the water. A similar reptile rose beside it. Then another, and another.

"Alligators!" Joe exclaimed.

"There must be a school of them!" Frank cried. "Come on, let's get out of here!"

He turned and climbed up the embankment. Joe started to follow him, but slipped in the mud. Wildly he flung his arms out in a desperate effort to maintain his balance. A hillock broke lose under his foot.

With a scream, Joe toppled into the river and was swept by the current toward the lethal reptiles!

CHAPTER XVI

Unexpected Revelation

ONE alligator spotted Joe in the water and eagerly moved toward him. Three others followed with open jaws!

Frantically Joe swam against the current. He was a strong athlete, but the swift-moving waves carried him downstream away from the bank. The alligators gained on him, slithering through the water like torpedoes!

Frank ran to a bend in the stream. He tore a long creeper from a tree and tossed one end far out into the water in his brother's path. Joe grabbed the creeper as he went past.

"Help—me!" he yelled.

Frank braced himself on the bank and tugged on the creeper. As he drew it in, Joe kicked his feet and began to move faster through the waves. But the alligators were still gaining on him!

As Joe reached the shallow water, Frank

dropped the creeper, held on to the tree branch with one hand, and extended the other out over the stream. Joe grabbed it and Frank pulled his brother up the bank.

A rasping crunch sounded just behind Joe. One of the alligators hurled itself out of the water in an effort to close its jaws on its prey. Missing by a hair's breath, the giant reptile splashed back into the waves.

Joe lay high on the bank, gasping for breath. "Frank," he panted, "you were better than the U.S. Cavalry galloping up to save the old homestead in the movies!"

"Well," Frank replied, "I figured that if you insisted on playing tag with a bunch of alligators, you might need help in a hurry."

When Joe recovered, the Hardys found that the bend in the stream carried it away from their starting point. Frank got a fix with his compass on a direct march through the jungle, and half an hour later the boys arrived at the pyramid.

Steve Weiss and Frank Pendleton had made sketches and layouts and were about ready to leave. "What happened to you?" Steve asked Joe, who was still wet from his swim.

"I was in a racing meet with some alligators," Joe said and told them about his adventure.

Steve shook his head. "Please don't pull any more stunts like that! We haven't had any casualties so far, and we'd like to keep our record clean."

When the group reached Palango, the Hardys showered and changed their clothes, then washed those they had worn and hung them up to dry in the late afternoon sun. Then they recounted their adventures to Chet, Biff, Tony, and Armstrong.

"Any news on this end?" Frank asked.

"Nothing," Biff said. "Tony and I inspected the surroundings now and then, but spotted no one."

Armstrong frowned. "I'm not surprised to hear that. I still think Calderón's guilty."

"What do you suggest we do?" Frank asked.

"Let's go back to Mexico City and check with the authorities."

Next morning the group thanked the people at the dig for their hospitality, then jeeped back to Mérida and took a plane to Mexico City. They found Mr. Hardy at the Montezuma Hotel, which he and John Armstrong had made their headquarters while staying in Mexico.

"Rumble Murphy has been indicted," he reported, "and the police have arrested his Mexico City contact, a man by the name of Hank Corda. But there's no evidence that they were involved with the Wakefield heist. What did you find out in Palango?"

Frank described the incident with Carlos

Calderón and the gold mask. He mentioned the suspicion that the young man had been hypnotized.

"That's possible," Fenton Hardy mused. "Hypnosis has been used before in crimes."

Armstrong stirred in his chair. "Calderón is our prime suspect! I want a thorough investigation of him. Take all the time you need. You've got to solve the Wakefield theft!"

The boys promised to get to work right away. First they went to the university and checked on Carlos. The administration confirmed that he was an archaeology student, top man in his class, and was doing work financed by the government. Carlos enjoyed the highest reputation in academic circles.

At police headquarters Frank and Joe were told that Carlos Calderón had no criminal record. The officer in charge made a call to the Department of Aviation to confirm that Calderón held a pilot's license.

"The story Carlos told us checks out," Frank advised his buddies as they walked toward a shop to have soft drinks.

"Does anybody think Carlos was working with Rumble Murphy?" Joe asked. "Frank and I doubt it."

Their friends agreed.

"What about Pedro Zemog?" Joe went on.

"Zemog took a gold horse. Carlos took a gold mask. Is there a connection?"

"We don't know enough about this guy Zemog," Biff commented.

Suddenly Frank sat up in his chair. He put his glass down so hastily that soda spilled over the rim onto the marble-topped table. "Zemog!" he exclaimed. "Ze-mog. I have an idea. Read it backwards!"

"G-o-m-e-z," Tony ticked off the letters.

"That's a popular Mexican name," Frank continued. "Maybe that's the real name of the man we're after. Come on, let's check the directory."

The boys went to a phone booth and Frank flipped the pages of the telephone book. He ran his finger down a column of names.

"Boy, Gomez is like Smith back home," he said. "And there are a lot of Pedros among them."

"We'll have to split up and take the names one at a time," Joe suggested.

Frank nodded and wrote two lists of names. He gave one to Biff, who would be accompanied by Chet and Tony. The Hardys took the second list.

They called on half a dozen men named Pedro Gomez. None was the person they were looking for. The seventh call took them to an apartment in the suburbs of Mexico City. Frank rang the bell. A man with gray hair opened the door. When he saw the Hardys, he tried to shut the door quickly, but Frank blocked it by placing his foot on the sill. "Pedro Gomez," he said sternly, "we want to talk to you. May we come in?"

Gomez opened the door. "All right. You might as well. I am tired of running."

They went into the apartment. Apparently Gomez was alone. He was nervous and shifted uneasily from one foot to the other.

"You will not find what you came to get," he told them in an unfriendly tone.

Frank and Joe were startled by the words.

"You admit you had it?" Joe asked incredulously.

"Of course I had it. But I have it no longer. I sold it a few days ago."

"You sold the Scythian figurine?" Frank exclaimed.

Now it was Gomez's turn to look startled. "The what?"

"The day you visited the museum in New York you stole the figurine of a rearing horse and ran off with it!" Frank reminded him.

"Oh, no! I did not steal the piece!"

Frank stared at the Mexican. "Come on, Mr. Gomez, we saw you running out of the place."

"Of course I ran. I was afraid for my life!"

"Why don't you tell us your version of the event?" Joe suggested.

The man nodded. "Yes. But I think you will not believe me."

"Try us."

Gomez said he had seen a tall blond man open the display case and take out the horse. When the man realized that Gomez had observed him, he hit the Mexican on the head and knocked him against the wall.

"When I got up, the blond man had left the room," Gomez said. "I ran out after him, but could not see him. Then I heard the guard shout and realized I would be the prime suspect. So I hurried out the door and luckily got a taxi right away."

Frank and Joe looked at each other. "A tall blond man!" Frank said. "That jibes with the description of the guard."

"But, Mr. Gomez," Joe said, "why do you travel under an alias?"

"I am a salesman of rare stamps. I must take every precaution when I travel."

"So that's what you had in your briefcase," Joe marveled. "The bulge we thought was the Scythian horse was actually a package of stamps."

Gomez nodded. "Unique Ruritanian issues, two hundred years old. Priceless! I thought you were trying to steal them from me. That is why I told you just now that I sold them. I did not know you were referring to the Scythian horse."

"What about the letters A.P.?" Frank asked. "We found two telegrams addressed to Pedro Zemog, and signed with those initials."

"They stand for Associated Philatelists," Gomez explained. "I represent the company that sends me buyers' orders by telegram when I am on the road. The first one told me to take the Ruritanian consignment to Zurich, but the Swiss buyer backed out at the last minute. Then I was told to go to my hometown of Mexico City, where a deal went through."

"You ran from us in Zurich because you thought we were after your stamps?" Joe asked.

Gomez nodded.

"And you used the name Jones at the hotel because you knew we had seen you on the plane?"

"Correct."

"Incidentally, were you in Chapultepec Castle the other day?"

Gomez smiled. "Yes. I saw you, and I knew you saw me. So I left."

"Have you ever been to Wakefield?"

"What?"

Joe described the gold heist at the mint.

"My friend," Gomez protested, "you have suspected me of two crimes that I did not commit!"

"My apologies," Joe said.

"Now then, who are you?" Gomez demanded.

"We're Americans from Bayport, Frank and Joe Hardy. We're investigating the thefts we told you about."

While Joe was talking to Gomez, Frank tried to reconstruct the scene at the museum. The guard had said he saw the tall blond man emerge from the Animal Chamber and bury his cigarette in the sand bucket. Maybe the man had hidden the figurine instead!

"Mr. Gomez," Frank said, "may I use your phone and call the Early Art Museum in New York? I'll pay you, of course."

"Go ahead."

Frank was connected with Orlov. Before he could say anything, the Russian curator gave a cry that Joe and Gomez could both hear.

"Finally you call!" he exclaimed. "Why have you not contacted me sooner?"

CHAPTER XVII

Hypnotized!

"We didn't have news for you until now," Frank said.

"News? I hope good news!"

"Yes. Look for the missing figurine in the sand bucket in the hallway."

"What? But—" Orlov put down the phone in confusion. A few minutes later he came back on. "You were right! This is fantastic. How did you know?"

"We found Zemog."

"Remarkable. He hid it there?"

"No. The tall blond man did. When he saw the guard, he put the horse in the sand bucket because he was afraid he'd be caught."

"You mean Zemog is not the thief?"

"No. He was an innocent bystander who saw what happened. The blond man hit him and knocked him against the wall. That's why he ran out of the building."

"Amazing, absolutely amazing! I am very happy about it. Thanks to you, good international relations have not been endangered, and I shall report on your good work to my government."

Orlov hung up. Frank told Gomez and Joe about the discovery of the Scythian figurine.

"That is a relief to me," Gomez said. "It proves once and for all that I am not the thief!"

"It sure does, Mr. Gomez," Frank agreed.

"If we ever need rare stamps," Joe said, "we'll give you a buzz."

The Hardys went back to the Montezuma Hotel and waited in the lobby for their pals. Chet, Biff, and Tony straggled in, looking worn out. Chet flopped down into an easy chair and ran his fingers through his hair. "I'm bushed!" he said.

"I'm disappointed," Tony stated. "Every Pedro Gomez we talked to was a false lead."

"Don't worry," Frank said. "We found the right one!"

After telling his friends about the rare-stamp salesman, Frank led the way to the room where Fenton Hardy and John Armstrong were discussing strategy.

"Carlos Calderón is clean," Frank said. "We also found Zemog. His real name is Gomez and he sells stamps. And—the gold horse never left the museum in New York."

"What!" Mr. Hardy exclaimed in surprise. "Tell us all about it."

When the boys had finished their account, Mr.

Hardy smiled. "Good detective work, boys. As far as the Mexican angle is concerned, I think we've exhausted it. We've been in touch with every conceivable agent dealing in gold, and nothing has turned up. I've also spoken with Johann Jung on the telephone just now, and he says the gold has not surfaced in Switzerland."

Armstrong put his head between his hands. "We're up against a stone wall!" he said in despair. "No leads whatsoever. But I still feel the solution lies here in Mexico."

"John, you can't go by a hunch. I vote we return to Wakefield and start from scratch."

Armstrong threw up his hands and sighed. "All right. At this point, I don't know what to do."

The group caught a jet for New York the next day. Chet, Biff, and Tony went back to Bayport, while the other four reached Wakefield in the evening. The Hardys checked into a motel, and Armstrong went home.

"I can't get this hypnosis business out of my mind," Joe confessed. "Who hypnotized Carlos? We know Murphy was in custody, and Gomez is on the level. Too bad Carlos couldn't remember anything."

Frank had an idea. "Wait a minute! That's what the guards at the mint said. They couldn't remember anything about the gold heist the night they were on duty. Maybe they were hypnotized, too!"

Mr. Hardy nodded. "Good thinking, Frank.

That would explain how they passed the lie-detector test. They could have let the thieves into the vault. And they could be telling the truth when they say they don't know a thing about it."

Frank and Joe were electrified by the theory.

"Who could have hypnotized the guards?" Joe asked.

"The same guy who hypnotized Carlos," Frank replied. "We were shadowed all the way from Wakefield to Palango. Look! The gang leader used hypnosis to steal the gold. If he came down to the dig, he could have worked on Carlos, too!"

"That's an involved theory," Fenton Hardy said. "And if you're right, chances are the man followed us back to Wakefield. We'll keep the mint under surveillance all day tomorrow and see what happens. Now let's get some sleep!"

The private investigator and his sons roomed together, but had separate beds. Mr. Hardy was next to the window and Frank near the door, with Joe in between. Exhausted from their long journey, they fell asleep at once.

Frank woke suddenly in the middle of the night. He had an uncanny feeling that something was wrong. "Probably a nightmare," he thought. Then he heard a scuffing noise and raised his head.

A ghostly figure glided across the room through the darkness, opened the door, and went out. The door clicked shut.

Frank noticed a slight sickish-sweet odor in the

room. It grew rapidly stronger. His head began to swim. His detective training warned him what was happening. He leaped out of bed, and opened the door wide. Joe, awakened by Frank's shout, threw all the windows up. Mr. Hardy lay still.

Coughing and choking, the boys pulled their father from his bed and propped him up with his head out one of the windows. They leaned over the other one, gasping for fresh air. Mr. Hardy began to breathe regularly again.

By the time he revived, the gas had dissipated. They all sat down on their beds and talked over their close call.

"It seems as if Frank's theory has merit," Mr. Hardy said. "Our enemy may have followed us back here, and now he wants to get us out of the way."

"But if the gold is already in Mexico or somewhere else, why would he get nervous because we're back in Wakefield?" Joe asked.

"He probably wouldn't. Which means, the gold must still be here!"

"He's sure determined to kill us," Frank said. "He's as dangerous as a rattlesnake!"

"I think one of us should keep watch for the rest of the night," Mr. Hardy said. "I'll do it."

"We'll take turns," Frank suggested.

"Don't worry about it," his father said. "Most of the night is already gone. You two go back to sleep. Someone has to be bright and alert in the morning."

*The boys pulled their father out of his bed and propped
him up with his head out the window.*

They bolted the door, but nothing more happened. After an early breakfast they took a circuitous route through the woods to the mint. Fenton Hardy dropped off near the front gate and concealed himself behind a clump of trees where he could watch the entrance without being seen. Frank and Joe slipped behind some bushes at the back of the building and kept vigil near the rear door and side exit.

Workers began arriving. They left their cars in the parking lot and entered the building. Then visitors streamed in.

"They don't know about the gold heist," Frank whispered.

"Armstrong has been keeping the theft under wraps," Joe observed.

Hours went by. The sun grew hot, and the Hardys felt cramped.

"I'm hungry," Frank said.

"I'll have a hot dog and a bottle of soda," said Joe, pretending to nibble on a weiner.

"Make mine a hamburger," Frank joked, "and a side order of French fries. I'd like to be in the Bayport Diner right now, Joe!"

"So would I," Joe said. "Surveillance is tough when you're hungry."

They took out some cookies they had brought with them and had their midday meal. Evening came, and the boys strained their eyes toward the rear gate of the mint but saw nothing suspicious.

Suddenly dry leaves snapped in the bushes behind them! The Hardys whirled around and got ready for action as the sound approached.

"I'll tackle him!" Frank whispered. "You clamp your hand over his mouth."

The noise grew louder, then stopped behind the nearest bush. The branches parted and a face peered through at them. It was that of a little black and white terrier!

The Hardys laughed and sat down in relief.

"A canine suspect," Joe chortled.

The dog advanced, wagging his tail. Frank stroked his back. Joe scratched his ears.

"Okay. Off you go," the boy said. The terrier rubbed his head against the young detective's arm and licked his hand. "Go home!" Frank commanded. Instead, the dog climbed into his lap, where he settled down.

The Hardys tried to push him away. Thinking they wanted to play, he rolled over and over, pawing the air in a friendly fashion.

"We must get rid of him," Frank muttered.

Joe found an extra cookie in his pocket. "This should do the trick," he said, chucking the cookie in a high arc over the bushes.

The terrier darted after the flying missile, and came back with the cookie in his mouth! The Hardys groaned as he laid it at Joe's feet.

Eagerly the animal looked up at him, wagging his tail, obviously asking for another chance to fetch the cookie. Getting no response, the dog began to whine.

Frank became alarmed. "If he starts barking, everybody in the mint will know we're here!"

Just then a small bearded man came through the back gate and headed in their direction. The Hardys were frantic with fear that the dog would give them away!

The bearded man came directly toward them, walking up to the bush they were hiding behind. The dog growled at him.

"That did it," Frank thought. "How are we going to explain?"

The man seemed to pay no attention, however. Instead of circling around the bush and confronting the boys, he veered to one side and walked into the woods without even looking at the dog.

"Joe! What do you make of that?" Frank asked, puzzled. "He didn't blink an eye!"

"I don't know," Joe said slowly, watching the man intently. "He—he's strolling along in a funny way, almost like a zombie!"

"Joe! Maybe he's been hypnotized. Let's follow him."

CHAPTER XVIII

The Big Discovery

THE bearded man walked rapidly through the woods. It was dark enough for Frank and Joe to follow him at a close distance. They were relieved when the terrier dropped behind and then ran off.

"I hope he's headed for home," Frank thought.

The man they were shadowing never looked behind or to either side as he went. He kept his right hand plunged into the pocket of his jacket as if protecting something. Reaching the dirt road Frank and Joe had scouted before, he avoided the road itself by moving through rough underbrush to the left.

"He doesn't want to be seen by anyone coming down the road," Frank murmured.

"I guess the guy who hypnotized that man told him to stay clear of it," Joe replied.

The stranger turned away from the road on a long hike through the woods to the empty airstrip, which he crossed. A plane could easily land or take off on it.

"Somebody's keeping the place ready to use," Frank said in an undertone.

"A plane could even be parked in the underbrush," Joe replied. "I wonder if the beard is meeting the pilot here."

Their quarry did not stop, however. He walked across the airstrip into the woods on the opposite side. He and his two shadows continued past tall trees whose bare branches were etched in sharp outlines against the night sky.

Soon they came to an old unused dirt road. In spite of the darkness, the boys could see two parallel furrows. A vehicle had recently been driven up the road.

They followed the man until he came to a barbed-wire fence with a wooden gate. The Hardys ducked into the underbrush and watched the stranger advance to the gate. Another man approached from the other side, cradling a rifle over his arm.

"Give the password," he demanded.

"Golden moonlight."

The gate was opened and the beard went through, disappearing around a bend. The guard sat down on a stump and placed his weapon across his knees as he resumed his vigil.

Frank tapped Joe on the shoulder. He pointed along the fence, indicating that they should scout in that direction. Stealthily the two boys crept through the underbrush past the guard. They followed the fence until they noticed a light shining through the trees. Moving closer, they saw the outline of a cavernous barn on the opposite side. The light came from a window, its beam falling upon a dusty pickup truck parked outside.

"We'd better investigate," Joe said, and he depressed the barbed wire with his foot. He put a hand on one of the fence posts and vaulted over. Frank followed, but his foot slipped and his jacket became entangled in the barbed wire!

"Joe!" he hissed. "I'm caught!"

His brother took off his own jacket, which he used to protect his hands as he pushed the barbed wire down. Frank pulled himself free and dropped down on the other side.

Slipping up to the area of the light, the Hardys hit the ground and crawled to the barn. Joe snaked his way around the pickup and Frank followed him. Then they peered into the barn window, which was ajar.

They saw an enormous room. A floor of broad planks extended from wall to wall. Dark rafters loomed overhead, and on either side of the room rickety stairs led to the haymow.

Each side of the building had a heavy reinforced wooden door fastened by a large bolt and chain. Peepholes had been cut in the doors so that anyone on the inside could identify visitors before admitting them.

Three men were seated at a table in the middle

of the barn under a single overhead light bulb, playing cards. They were a rough-looking threesome with two days' growth of beard on their faces. Two wore levis and plaid shirts. The man who seemed to be their leader was dressed in slacks and in a turtleneck sweater.

Turtleneck dealt the cards. Each man picked up his hand and looked at it. One of the plaids started his bet and threw some chips into the pot.

As Frank and Joe surveyed the scene, their eyes focused in a corner that gave off a golden glow.

Gold bars lay stacked on top of one another!

"Maybe that's the gold from the Wakefield Mint!" Joe gasped.

Frank nodded as the betting at the table continued. Turtleneck drew in the pot, adding a stack of chips to those he already had.

"I'm having lousy luck," one of his companions said. "I want a new deck of cards."

Turtleneck glared at him. "You accusing Jake Slobodky of cheating? You saying I just dealt from the bottom of the deck?"

"Naw," the man replied. "I'm just saying my luck might change with a new deck."

The game continued. Jake won again. He grinned as he raked in the chips.

The third man slammed his cards down in disgust.

"You complaining about how I deal, too?" Jake demanded.

"I'm complaining about this waiting," the man grumbled. "We've got the gold here. The plane's ready. Let's get this show on the road!"

"You calling the shots now?" Jake asked.

"No, but I got a stake in this operation. And if you want my opinion, I say—"

A loud knock on the door interrupted him. The three men jumped to their feet and tiptoed to the door, where the pair in plaid shirts flattened themselves against the wall. Jake opened the peephole and looked out.

"Give the password!" he ordered.

"Golden moonlight."

"Okay. Come on in."

Jake unfastened the chain and shot back the bolt. The beard entered. His eyes were wide open and his face expressionless.

"He looks just the way Carlos did," Joe thought.

The beard still had his right hand deep in his pocket. He stopped inside the door as if rooted to the spot. The other three gathered around him expectantly.

Jake spoke loudly to him, emphasizing each word. "What is your mission?"

"I must deliver the message," the man said in a weird voice that seemed to come from a great distance.

"What is the message?"

"I do not know."

"Where is the message?"

"I have it here." He drew his hand out of his pocket. He was clutching a piece of paper in a tight grasp.

"Give me the message," Jake ordered. "And then return to your home."

The man handed the paper to him, did an about face, went through the door, and walked down the road toward the gate. Jake locked the door. "The trance works," he chortled. "That guy'll be dead to the world till he wakes tomorrow morning. And he won't remember coming out here. Just like the guards who let us heist the gold from the vault."

"But this man was able to talk. I don't like it," one of the plaids objected.

"Nothing to worry about. He's programmed to answer just the questions I asked. If the Hardys catch him, he won't spill the beans." Jake held the paper up to the light under the table.

"Wow!" he exploded. "Tomorrow is D-Day! The plane arrives at midnight and we'll be airborne pretty soon and got to be ready to move. Hey, gang, we're gonna be rich!"

After the general excitement had died down, the men started another game of cards. Jake won again. "This is my lucky day!" he boasted.

Frank nudged Joe. "They know we're on their trail," he whispered.

"But they don't know how close we are," Joe

replied. "Think we should go and let Dad know?"

"Not yet," Frank advised. "Jake and his pals are small-time crooks. Let's stay and see if we can find out who the ringleader is."

"Good idea."

The card game ended, and the players rose to their feet. Jake stretched and rubbed the back of his neck. "Might as well hit the hay," he announced.

"That's not so easy to do," the big loser grumbled. "The haymow's full of hay and dust. What a place for us to be holed up!"

"We'll use the cots in the corner, as usual," Jake said, "and it'll be for the last time."

Click! A rifle bolt had suddenly slipped into place. Frank and Joe whirled around. They found themselves staring into the business end of a shotgun!

CHAPTER XIX

Captured!

THE guard who had been standing at the gate was looking through the sight of his rifle. The Hardys were caught! The man lowered his weapon and gave them a wolfish grin. "Okay, wise guys. We'll take care of you. We don't like snoopers around here. Get going and keep your hands where I can see them. Move!"

Frank and Joe started walking. The guard prodded them with his rifle. "Reach for the sky and hurry up. No funny business!"

He forced the boys around the corner of the barn to one of the doors and knocked three times in rapid succession. The peephole opened. Jake peered through suspiciously. "What's up?" he growled.

"We got visitors."

"Well, well. Bring them in!"

Jake opened the door, and the man with the gun forced the Hardys inside the barn.

"I found them eavesdropping at the window," he explained. "Figured you might want me to introduce them to you."

"You figured right!" Jake snapped. "How long have they been there?"

"Long enough!"

"Good going, Sam. If anybody else sneaks up to the barn, bring them in too. These guys may have confederates."

"Right." Sam left. Jake bolted the door.

The two men in plaid shirts were armed. They glowered at Frank and Joe while Jake started the interrogation.

"All right," he snarled. "What do you mean by sneaking around here?"

The Hardys tried to bluff their way through the predicament in which they found themselves.

"We were hiking through the woods near here," Frank said. "We didn't know about the barn until we saw the light through the trees."

"We were hungry," Joe added, "and came to see if we could grub a meal."

The three men laughed in a sinister manner. "Oh sure," Jake sneered. "You just happened to be spying on us through the window. You punks had better talk—and fast!"

Frank and Joe remained silent. They were playing for time. Their captors scowled at them.

"Talk won't do any good," one of the plaid-shirted men said. "We've got to do them in. They've seen the gold."

The other supported him. "They know too much. Let's deep six 'em, now!"

Amazement gripped Frank and Joe. Those were the words on the note Joe had found in the abandoned car at the airstrip!

The speaker misunderstood their reaction. "So, that scares you, does it? Well, it should. We mean business!" He moved toward Joe, and his companions walked up to Frank. The Hardys braced themselves.

Then Jake stopped. "We have to wait for Mr. Big. Maybe he'll want to talk to them. Let's tie these guys up and sit tight until he gets here. It won't be long."

The men pushed the Hardys into a corner, made them sit down with their backs to the wall, produced rope, and tied their hands behind their backs.

The crooks returned to their card game. Frank and Joe sat side-by-side with the ropes chafing their wrists and conversed in whispers.

"Joe, nobody knows we're here," Frank said. "Too bad we didn't have a chance to alert Dad before we followed the beard."

"Right. We'll have to get out of this on our own," Joe replied.

Three quick knocks sounded on the door, followed by three slow ones, then the three fast ones were repeated. The men at the card table leaped to their feet.

"Mr. Big!" Jake exclaimed. "That's his signal. Get ready, and don't talk out of turn."

He unbolted the door without looking through the peephole, and swung it open. Mr. Big entered.

The Hardys gasped. *John Armstrong*, the administrative assistant of the Wakefield Mint walked into the room!

"Everything in order, Jake?" he asked.

"Sure thing, boss. Except a couple of prowlers came sneaking around the barn."

"Prowlers?" Armstrong sounded alarmed.

"Don't worry, boss. We caught 'em and we've got 'em."

"Where are they?"

"Over there." Jake pointed to the corner where the two captives were tied up.

Armstrong threw up his hands in astonishment. "Don't you know who they are?" he demanded.

"Should I?" Jake queried.

"Well, maybe not. They're Frank and Joe Hardy!"

"Fenton Hardy's sons?" Jake squinted uneasily. "That means the gumshoe is on to us."

Armstrong shook his head. "Hardy doesn't know anything about our operation. And these two don't matter any more." He advanced toward Frank and Joe. "Fooled you, didn't I?" he asked slyly.

"You sure did," Frank admitted. "First you steal the gold. Then you send us on a wild goose chase to Switzerland by spreading the rumor that the gold will be sold there."

"It would have been sufficient if my friend Rudolf Kling hadn't picked a loser like Pfeiffer to do the talking," Armstrong growled.

Frank nodded. "Pfeiffer was caught in a burglary. And when we left Zurich after that, you sent us to Mexico by dreaming up the clue of the airplane, then insisted on traveling to Palango with Dad to get us and him as far as possible from Wakefield. The gold was here all the time."

Armstrong agreed. "The guy I had hired to fly it out gave me trouble on the time schedule. That's why I had to keep you occupied in distant places. Then the idiot got himself arrested in Mexico City just before we came back. But I got a replacement for him, who'll do the job tonight and—"

Frank interrupted him. "Your pilot was arrested? Is his name Hank Corda?"

"Right. I didn't know about his connection with Murphy. He had Corda's name and address on him, and when he was booked the cops found it. That was all I needed! But I fixed it. This is the final case for Frank and Joe Hardy. We're going to drop you into the sea from our plane and this time tomorrow you'll be playing with the fishes in the Caribbean!"

The ringleader turned toward his henchmen. "Forget about these boys," he said. "Our plane arrives around midnight. The pilot wants this to be a quick job. So do I."

"Everything is ready, boss."

Armstrong walked over to the gold bars, picked one off the top, and looked at it. It glittered in the glare of the overhead bulb.

"That's a beautiful sight," he said. "I haven't seen these since they were in the vault at the mint. I was at home when the theft took place, if you recall."

Jake grinned. "Best alibi anyone ever had."

Armstrong looked pleased. "I think so. Well, these bars have come a long way to get to this barn. From Siberia to Moscow to Zurich to Wakefield. Next stop—an uninhabited island in the Caribbean. We divide the loot there and go our separate ways. If we ever meet again, we don't know one another." Armstrong put the bar back on the pile. "Say, how have you fellows been killing time out here?"

"Playing cards," Jake replied.

"How about dealing me in?"

"Sure thing, boss."

Armstrong occupied the fourth chair at the table. Jake dealt the hands and the game began.

Frank gently tried to pull his wrists apart. He felt a slight give in the ropes. Tapping Joe's foot with his, he leaned toward his brother. "I may be able to untie myself," he whispered. "How about you?"

Joe tested his own bonds. "Not a chance."

Twisting his right wrist against his left, Frank felt the rope stretch. He explored with his fingers until they closed over the knot. Using his escape technique, he figured out how the knot had been tied and rubbed it between his thumb and finger. Gingerly he tugged at the shorter strand.

It moved. Little by little, in an agonizingly slow process, Frank drew the shorter strand loose. His hands were free! He sat still for a moment, watching the card game. All four players were intent on the betting as the pot grew larger and larger.

Frank pressed his shoulder against Joe's to hide his fingers, which were working on his brother's bonds. The second rope fell away and Joe was released.

"They may not notice us," Frank whispered, "if we sneak up into the haymow, go out the window, and shimmy down the drainpipe."

"What about the guy at the gate?" Joe asked.

"We'll worry about him when we get there. The first thing is to get out. Come on!"

The Hardys rose slowly to their feet, never taking their eyes off the card game. They tiptoed over to the stairs. Frank led the way up step by step. As he placed his foot on the top rung, it creaked loudly.

The noise cut through the stillness of the huge barn, setting up echoes in the rafters. Startled,

Armstrong swiveled in his chair and looked for its source. He spotted Joe's feet at the top of the stairs.

"The Hardys are loose!" he cried angrily. "After them! Don't let them get away!"

The other three men scrambled to their feet, tipping over the chairs in their haste. They pounded across the floor to the stairs.

Now that their escape had been discovered, Frank and Joe plunged forward into the haymow. The atmosphere was hot, the air was dusty, and the hay was slippery. The boys leaped to the right behind a high pile of hay. Staying low, they ran toward the opposite end of the haymow, slipping and sliding all the way.

Footsteps pounded up the stairs, and Jake and his two henchmen climbed into the loft.

"Where are they?" Jake bellowed.

Seeing no movement, he led the way to the left side, where clear boards offered easier footing. Frank and Joe saw them go past, and jumped into the middle of the hay, believing they could cross over and reach the stairs.

But Joe's feet shot out from under him. He skidded on the hay—right into Jake, who had doubled back. The unexpected collision caused Jake to tumble into a large haypile. He coughed, wheezed, and sneezed, then came up with wisps of dry weeds sticking from his hair. Before he could extricate himself, Frank and Joe ran down the left side while the other two pursuers came up on the right.

A tall pole near the stairs at the far end of the loft reached up to a crossbeam. Frank shimmied up the pole onto the crossbeam, and Joe followed instantly. The brothers perched where they could look all the way across the haymow.

"I hope they think we went downstairs," Frank muttered.

The three men gathered beneath them, panting, swearing, and looking around furiously. "They got to be up here!" Jake snarled. "We don't go down till we find where they're hiding!"

"Which way?" said a plaid-shirted searcher. "Left or right?"

"Left, right, up, and down! Look everywhere."

The Hardys were sure to be discovered. Frank signaled Joe. Balancing themselves on the crossbeam, they hurtled down simultaneously, hitting the three men across the shoulders and knocking them down in a heap. Then the boys dived for the stairs, and jumped down three steps at a time. When they reached the bottom, however, they ran straight into the muzzle of a gun!

"Okay, wise guys," Armstrong said. "The jig is up!"

CHAPTER XX

In the Nick of Time

As Armstrong gave his command, the Hardys froze in their tracks and raised both hands over their heads. Footsteps pounded down the stairs behind them.

"Nice going, boss," Jake called out.

"Tie them up again," Armstrong ordered, "and this time see that they stay that way!"

Frank and Joe were hustled over to a corner and bound with ropes around their wrists and ankles. Jake tested the knots.

"Don't worry," he said. "These guys will stick around till we move them."

"Good," Armstrong said. "All we have to do is take them with us and unload them from the plane at five thousand feet. By the way, you'd better bolt the barn door again."

Jake walked to the entrance and reached for the bolt. *Wham!* The door burst open, the edge striking Jake and knocking him off his feet!

Fenton Hardy stepped into the barn, followed by the Wakefield chief of police and a number of officers. "Drop the gun, Armstrong!" the detective commanded.

Armstrong hesitated for a second, then the rifle clattered to the floor. The police disarmed his henchmen, who sullenly refused to say anything.

"We'd like to join the party," Joe called out, "but we're tied up."

Fenton Hardy walked over and unfastened the ropes. "Are you all right?" he asked.

"Fine," Frank replied. "But we wouldn't have been for long. These men were going to let us take a long-distance swan dive into the Caribbean."

"You got here just in the nick of time," Joe said, relieved.

Armstrong swung around at the words. "Hardy," he grated, "how did you figure out my little scheme?"

"It hit me while I was keeping the front gate of the mint under surveillance. The guards at the mint had been hypnotized. And from the way my sons described Carlos Calderón, he, too, must have been in a trance."

"We wondered who did it," Frank put in, "but never guessed the truth."

"Neither did I, Frank," Mr. Hardy said. "For the longest time I suspected a third person who might have tailed us to Mexico. Yet Armstrong had the opportunity to hypnotize both the guards and Carlos! Of course, the theory seemed ridiculous. The administrative assistant to the director robbing his own mint! Nevertheless, I decided to shadow him, and it paid off."

"Dad, why didn't you let us know?" Joe asked.

"By the time I realized all this, you two had left your post at the rear gate of the mint. I presume you had good reason?"

Frank described how they had seen the hypnotized man with the beard and decided to follow him.

"Good thinking," Mr. Hardy said. "Anyway, I went to a pay phone and called Chief Erikson, and he came on the run with his men to help me make this arrest."

"Glad to round them up, Fenton," Erikson replied. "I know how often you've been right about criminals."

Mr. Hardy turned to Armstrong. "We saw you come out of the mint. You didn't know it, but you had a police escort every step of the way through the woods to the barn."

"We collared the man with the rifle at the gate," the chief took up the story. "Then we came up the road and watched the action in the barn for a while."

"You took a chance, Erikson," Armstrong declared. "As Hardy just said, the hypnotism theory was just a hunch. If you had made a mistake, I could have had your badge."

Erikson shook his head. "Not really. You see,

I come from Chicago, and I remember a stage hypnotist who called himself the Great Gordino. His pitch was to call for volunteers from the audience. He'd put them in a trance and make them perform odd antics, like playing leapfrog onstage, and so on. The Great Gordino got into trouble. He bet on the horses, lost heavily, and disappeared from the windy city one jump ahead of the sheriff."

"What was his real name?" Joe asked.

"John Armstrong! I never connected Gordino with the Wakefield Armstrong until your father told me he suspected this man of being a hypnotist. Then I was sure. I felt we should go all out after this suspect."

Armstrong caved in. "Sure, I was Gordino in Chicago before I arrived in Wakefield and got a job at the mint. And I had debts. Then I became greedy and wanted some of this gold."

"So you figured out a way to rob the mint?" Frank prodded him.

"I took a vacation in the Caribbean last winter. When I met Hank Corda, I made a deal with him. He put me in touch with Jake, who, with his men, cut the airstrip in the woods."

Jake glared at Armstrong, but did not deny the charges.

"Then you hypnotized the mint guards, told them to turn off the alarm system and the cameras, and to let Jake in," Frank deduced.

Armstrong nodded. "It worked like a charm. I'm still a pretty good hypnotist."

"You're a pretty good actor, too," Fenton Hardy said. "You fooled me completely when you engaged me to handle the case. And here you were simply using me to divert suspicion from yourself."

"Of course. If anyone asked me what I was doing about the gold heist, I could say I hired the famous private investigator from Bayport to run down the clues. But you ran down too many, Hardy!"

"Why did you have our father kidnapped?" Joe asked.

"Because he brought you into the act. That spoiled my plans because with that many people working on the case, it became too dangerous. So we wanted to get him out of the way before he could tell you anything he might have found out."

"But when he escaped," Frank said, "you left the note instructing your men to deep six F.H. in the glove compartment of the car used to transport the gold to the barn. You were giving Jake his orders."

Armstrong nodded. "Jake didn't like this, so I tried to keep you all away until the gold was safely out of this country."

Joe turned to his father. "He sent us to Zurich and had the rumor spread about the Wakefield gold being sold there," he said. "When that didn't keep us there long enough, he dreamed up the clue about the plane with 'Mexico City' on it."

Mr. Hardy chuckled. "It must have been a surprise for you, John, when we actually found such a plane."

"It fit right into his plans," Frank put in.

"So you hypnotized Carlos Calderón in Palango to have another suspect who would take up our time," Mr. Hardy said to Armstrong. "And when we came back to Wakefield earlier than it suited you, you gassed us in the motel. It was all part of your plot!"

Armstrong became angry. "Nothing would have happened to you if you had listened to me! Why wouldn't you stay in Mexico? When you refused, I had no alternative!"

Frank chuckled. "You probably figured you had everything under control when you came out to the barn tonight. You must have been surprised to see Joe and me trussed up like a couple of chickens ready for the spit!"

"Armstrong, your pilot will get a surprise, too," Fenton Hardy said. "The police will have a welcoming committee waiting for him when he lands at the airstrip."

"The getaway plane is due very soon," Frank reported. "We heard Armstrong say at about midnight."

"Put a stakeout at the airstrip at once," Erikson

directed his lieutenant. "Impound the plane, bring in the pilot, and have these prisoners taken away."

"Would you also call the Zurich police and have them arrest a man named Rudolf Kling," Frank added. "He was Armstrong's accomplice, who hired Pfeiffer to spread the rumor about the gold being sold in Switzerland."

Armstrong, Jake, and their two henchmen were led out in handcuffs. Mr. Hardy and Erikson walked over to the corner where the gold was stacked. The boys joined them. The bright shimmer of the bars dazzled them, and the hammer and sickle imprint was clearly visible.

"I've always wanted to know what a million in gold looked like," the police chief confided. "Now I do."

"If Armstrong's plan had succeeded, it would have been one of the century's most notorious crimes," Fenton Hardy observed.

"But it failed, thanks to you Hardys," Erikson pointed out. "By the way, Director Wadsworth of the mint returned from his vacation today. He's upset about the whole thing and will be relieved to hear that you've solved the case."

"I'll bet he won't be pleased to hear who the culprit is," Frank said.

"True. On the other hand, the three guards who were arrested are vindicated now and will be back at their jobs soon."

The gold bars were loaded into the pickup, and two officers guarded them while a third took the wheel. Chief Erikson gave the Hardys a lift to their motel.

The following morning Mr. Hardy spoke to Director Wadsworth on the telephone. He confirmed that the pilot had been arrested and thanked Mr. Hardy profusely for his help.

"I would never have suspected John Armstrong," the director said with a sigh. "I trusted him completely. Well, I'm glad he hired *you* to recover the gold."

The Hardys packed their bags and were soon on their way to Bayport. Frank felt a little disappointed, as he usually did when they wound up a case and the excitement was over. He did not anticipate their next thrilling adventure, *Mystery of the Firebird Rocket*.

When they arrived home, they were greeted anxiously by Mrs. Hardy and Aunt Gertrude.

"I'm so glad to see you," Mr. Hardy said. "Is everything all right?"

"Everything is great!" Joe replied with a grin.

"I'm sure it was dangerous," Aunt Gertrude put in.

"Oh no, Aunty, it was no trouble at all. By the way, we brought you a souvenir."

"Yes? What is it?"

"You have a choice. Either a jaguar god or a feathered serpent!"

DETACH ALONG DOTTED LINE AND MAIL IN ENVELOPE WITH PAYMENT